Love

It Was Never Meant For Me

...A Journey Through Broken Promises and Undying Hope!

Kulbhushan
Chaudhary (KK)

INDIA • SINGAPORE • MALAYSIA

ISBN

Hardcase 979-8-89724-548-2
Paperback 979-8-89632-836-0

This Book is a Dedication

To my wife,
Who once brought light and meaning to my life.

Though you have chosen a path apart,
Your presence shaped who I am today,
And the memories of what we shared will forever linger in my heart.

This book is not just a story;
It's a testament to love, loss, and resilience.
Even in your absence, your impact remains,
A bittersweet reminder of a chapter closed, yet unforgettable.

And should you ever find your way back,
Know that the door remains open,

Waiting for you to step in once again.

Contents

Preface

To all the true lovers, the ones who have given every piece of their heart, soul, and dreams to someone who never looked back—

This book is for you.

It is a journey into the depths of love that is pure, relentless, and brave—the kind of love that shows us what it means to be selfless, even in the face of heartbreak. It's about the nights spent awake, staring into the emptiness where once there was laughter, wondering how someone who once made you feel whole could leave so silently, so suddenly. It's for those of you who held onto hope when everything around seemed to fade, who believed in forever even when the other half of your heart didn't.

Here, you'll find pages filled with the sorrows and joys of unrequited love, moments that capture the breathtaking highs and shattering lows of loving someone more than they could ever understand. I hope that as you read, you'll feel seen, understood, and comforted in a way that only words can offer. And perhaps, through these stories and sentiments, you'll come to realize that love—even the kind that ends in heartbreak—is never truly wasted.

Every chapter we spend loving another, even if it goes unreturned, becomes part of our own journey, shaping us into beings capable of boundless love and resilience.

For those who have loved deeply and lost, may this book be a gentle reminder that you are not alone and that your love, though unreciprocated, was and always will be enough. This is for the ones who kept holding on when others let go and, in the process, discovered a well of strength within themselves that no one could ever take away.

This is for you.

Thank You!

As I take a step into sharing my story with you, I am filled with immense gratitude and love. First and foremost, I bow to the feet of Lord Saibaba, my mother, my family, and my brother-in-law, whose constant love, support, and belief in me have been the foundation on which this journey was built. Your unwavering presence in my life is my strength, and I owe everything to you.

"In broken pieces, I found my pen,
With scars as ink, I wrote again.
From the ashes of us, I built this rhyme,
A story of love in lost time."

I also extend my heartfelt thanks to my friends—Ankur, Sheetal, Ruhani, Deepankur, Dheeraj, Rohit, and Senthil. You all have been my shield, standing guard through every storm, silently protecting me when I felt vulnerable during the toughest times. With you, I found laughter, solace, and the freedom to express myself fully, especially during the making of this book. Our conversations, our shared moments, and your undying support made all the difference.

A special mention goes to my office colleagues—Nishant, Deepika, Amit, Aashish, Nancy, Tushan, Sunil, Sidhant, Saurabh, Preeti, Pankaj, Aakash, and many others. Your enthusiasm, encouragement, and the energy you brought into my life pushed me forward to keep writing, even when I doubted myself. You were the motivation that kept me going, and for that, I am forever grateful.

A special note of thanks to Amit Thakur and Akash Vajpai, my lawyers, who stood by my side during the toughest of times. Your unwavering support and guidance have been a pillar of strength, and I couldn't have navigated those challenges without you.

To my beacon of light, my heartbeat, my strength, my reason to smile, my son Inesh Kakker. Thank you for standing by me, for always being there, and for helping me find the missing pieces in my story. Your sharp eyes and thoughtful suggestions made this book whole, and I can never thank you enough. Your joy has kept me going, reminding me that even in the darkest times, there is always a reason to keep pushing forward.

Lastly, I want to extend my sincere gratitude to the entire team at Notion Press and V Spark Communications. Your belief in me and your hard work made this dream a reality, and for that, I will forever be thankful.

May God bless all of you, and may you always find the same love, strength, and peace that you have given me in abundance.

Thank you all for giving me the courage to transform fragments into this finished book. Hope you enjoy this book: Love - It was never meant for me.

"Love taught me how to heal others, but left me with wounds no one could see."

Chapter 1

The Heart of an Ordinary Dreamer

Kulbhushan aka KK, to anyone passing by, was just another middle-class boy from Delhi, the kind you'd walk past without a second glance. His life was a small one, bound by the familiar rhythm of simplicity: home, school, repeat. There were no grand adventures or dreams of city lights—just the quiet, repetitive hum of a world that seldom changed.

KK's family hailed from a farming background in Himachal Pradesh and shifted to Delhi for better prospects. His was as modest as they came, with love and sacrifice woven into the fabric of every day. They were three siblings: his elder sister, a gentle force always pushing herself to excel; KK, a quiet, unassuming presence; and his younger brother, the family's baby with a spark in his eyes that made everyone smile. Their father, a man of few words and boundless pride, wanted nothing more than to give his children the opportunities he never had.

His father was determined to see them succeed, irrespective of the sacrifices it demanded. Though his own English was limited, he'd spent every rupee he could spare to put his children in the best English-medium school he could find. It was his greatest wish that they would someday speak the language fluently, enter rooms where he'd never been invited, and leave behind the limitations he'd quietly borne his whole life. He'd tell them, "You'll go places I only ever dreamed of," his voice filled with a longing for a life he'd never have but one he desperately wanted for them.

Their mother was the heart of the family, holding them all together in ways unseen. Her suits were often worn out, faded with years of wear and countless washings, but she wore them with a quiet dignity that was uniquely hers. And even when life was hard, she was never without her dupatta. KK always believed that the dupatta was a magic shield. It wrapped around them like an embrace, shielding them from all the world's cruelty and hardships, as if every fiber of it was woven with love and resilience. In the hardest of times, that worn, familiar fabric became a blanket of hope, a promise that even when they had little, they had love.

Growing up in this house, KK learned early on that dreams were luxuries reserved for others. His family valued hard work, loyalty, and honesty above all else. They taught him that true wealth was not in material possessions but in a heart that could withstand life's storms and in hands willing to give. In their small house, there was no room for selfishness or entitlement, but only the endless, everyday sacrifices that kept their world running.

But even in his simple world, KK held a treasure—his heart. A heart unguarded, capable of kindness, and honesty that most would overlook. Though average by many standards—average in studies, average in looks, and sometimes even invisible to his classmates—he held within him a purity that made him unique, a golden heart that always wanted to heal, to help, to love.

Yet, if there was one person KK loved more than anything in the world, it was his mother. She was his anchor, his confidence, his everything. He knew her days were long, her nights even longer, yet she always found a way to smile, as if the entire world were a weight she could carry just to see him happy. KK felt that his love for her was like sunlight, something that warmed him from the inside and made him want to be a better person. To KK, she wasn't just his mother; she was the heartbeat of his entire world, the quiet strength that kept their small family stitched together.

Some nights, when the world was quiet, he would silently watch her doing household work. He'd watch the soft glow of the lamp highlight the lines on her face, lines that told stories of patience, of sacrifices no one ever thanked her for. KK promised himself that one day, he'd make her proud, give her back the life she'd given him, filled with all the quiet dreams she had put aside for his future. But for now, his love for her was his gift, his offering, something that shaped every choice he made.

While other boys of his age sought thrills or success, KK found joy in small, almost invisible moments. He was a dreamer in his own quiet way, a boy who wore his heart on his sleeve, no matter how much it hurt. He'd give his mother an embarrassed smile when he brought home grades just barely above passing, and she'd ruffle his hair with a proud, "You'll do better next time." His father would say little, only nodding, but KK could see the quiet pride in his eyes. To them, their children were their entire world, and that was enough for him.

Life for KK was about respect, loyalty, and truth—principles that his parents held close and that KK absorbed like air. He had never lied to them, not once. He respected them in a way that felt like love itself, feeling deeply that honesty was the only thing he could give in return for the life they'd built for him. Even when his friends bragged about skipping school or doing things their parents didn't know about, KK stayed silent. He couldn't imagine deceiving the people who had given him everything.

As the middle child, KK carried a responsibility he couldn't quite name—a duty to honor both his elder sister's dedication and his younger brother's innocence. His sister was the ambitious one, always pushing to prove herself, while his younger brother brought laughter to their family in a way only a child could. KK lived in the quiet space between them, absorbing the weight of expectations and the desire to be a steady presence his family could count on.

In school, KK's classmates paid him little attention. He wasn't the brightest, nor the most popular. He didn't have the quick wit to charm others or the looks to attract attention. Instead, he was often overlooked, his gentle nature misunderstood as meekness. Yet, he didn't resent his quiet life; he accepted it. It was part of who he was, part of the world he knew. KK's friends—few though they were—saw him as a stable, trustworthy figure, someone who never asked for much, yet gave all he had.

But KK's heart was what made him different. He wasn't like the other boys who pursued fame or success; he sought meaning. He wanted to be the kind of person who left others better than he'd found them, even if no one else ever knew his name. He'd often wonder if there would ever be someone who would see his heart for what it truly was—a heart willing to give everything, a soul untouched by the cynicism that often tainted those around him.

And so, KK carried on, walking through life with quiet grace, a heart unguarded and ready to love, even when he was unsure if anyone would ever love him back. But if there was one constant, one truth in his world, it was his love for his mother, a love woven into his very being, like a thread that could never break.

In his simple life, he hadn't yet known heartbreak, but he had already known the beauty of a heart willing to give everything. This was KK, a boy who dreamed quietly, a boy with a heart too pure for this world, waiting for a love he'd give everything to find.

* * * * *

Chapter 2

Echoes of a First Love

It all started with a shift—a gentle nudge from the familiar into the unknown. KK found himself moving from a well-known school, where dreams were often whispered among the stars, to a medium-grade school closer to home. The transition felt like a quiet storm, a reminder that life does not always follow the grand plans we set in our hearts. He had always been an average student, and his 10th board examination results reflected that—a stark reminder that sometimes, despite our best efforts, we falter. With scores that kept him from opting for Commerce with Maths, he was left with no choice but to embrace this new path.

Though it felt like a setback, KK promised himself it would be different this time. He vowed to focus more on his studies, to grasp the mathematical figures that spun the wheel of life. No longer would he be just an average student; he was determined to rise, to thrive. As the weeks passed, a transformation took place. Where once he struggled, he now excelled, becoming studious and dedicated. He topped the class, his name echoing in the hallways like a gentle wind, and even found time to participate in sports, discovering a joy in teamwork that fueled his spirit.

Amidst this blossoming, a girl named Nisha began to notice him. Her eyes sparkled with curiosity as she observed his simplicity and dedication. They quickly became good friends, sharing laughter and warmth in the school corridors. Their time together was filled with shared stories, dreams, and the comforting knowledge that they cared for one another. As they navigated the complexities of adolescence, their connection deepened, blossoming into a bond that felt almost sacred.

Their accounts teacher, a stern figure who wielded a scale with merciless authority, added an air of tension to their daily routine. KK watched his classmates cringe as they received stinging reprimands for missing homework or for faltering in class. The fear of a strike from the scale was a collective nightmare, a dark cloud hanging over the classroom. In the midst of this, KK became an unexpected beacon of light—an average-looking guy with a face dotted by pimples was now the center of attention. His new-found success in academics positioned him as a trusted friend, someone who would help his classmates with their homework and share insights on complex problems.

As KK settled into this new rhythm, he quickly realized that the world of friendship was far richer than he had ever imagined. Every day after school, he and Nisha would walk home together, their conversations a delightful mix of banter and serious talk. They would share their dreams and fears, and in the comforting silence of each other's company, they discovered a sense of belonging.

Each moment felt like a brushstroke on the canvas of their young lives, painting a picture of innocence and hope.

It was during one of their daily walks that Nisha gathered her courage and spoke her heart. "You should share your feelings, KK. Don't hold back," she urged gently, her voice a melody that danced through the air.

KK's heart raced. He wanted to speak the truth, to let her know how he felt, but insecurity gripped him. He worried about the potential fallout of letting feelings seep into their precious friendship. The fear of ruining what they had loomed like a shadow in his mind. Still, love has a way of making itself known, and it wasn't long before Nisha broke her silence, confessing that she had fallen for him.

In that moment, time stood still. KK felt an explosion of joy and fear intertwined within him. He had the same feelings for her but wanted to ensure that their studies wouldn't suffer due to their blossoming affection. "I like you too, but we need to focus on our studies," he stammered, his cheeks burning with shyness. He didn't want to accept or reject; instead, he remained silent, hoping to shield their friendship from the storm of young love. But Nisha was not deterred; she could see the truth shining in his eyes, and their connection deepened as they navigated the complexities of adolescent love.

Days turned into weeks, and their bond continued to flourish. Whenever KK was absent from school, Nisha would complete his homework and ensure his notebooks were filled with the work he'd missed, protecting him from the wrath of their accounts teacher. "You can't let them beat you, KK," she'd say with a teasing smile. "I won't let that happen." She embodied the kind of friendship that was both nurturing and playful, offering KK a safe haven amidst the pressures of school.

KK, in turn, made sure to help her with her work whenever she was unwell; their partnership became a beautiful dance of support. Their mutual trust and understanding grew, and soon they were appointed class monitors, a role that granted them more time together.

Every shared glance and whispered secret felt like a page from a dream, and for KK, it was as if he had been accepted for who he truly was. Nisha had seen beyond the surface, and she made him feel cherished. They would sit together during breaks, sharing their lunch as they talked about their aspirations, the future, and the little things that made them smile.

Evenings were often filled with phone calls where Nisha would playfully complain to KK's family about his naughtiness in class, making everyone laugh. KK never shied away from the truth; he confessed to his family that both he and Nisha liked each other, their hearts yearning for a shared future. "I like her, and I think she likes me," he would say with a shy grin, his mother's eyes sparkling with delight at the thought of young love.

Like the moon embraces the night,
Your laughter chases away my fright.
In the simplest moments, we find our way,
Two hearts dancing in the light of day.

Together, they crafted a story filled with sweet laughter, tender secrets, and a bond that promised a beautiful tomorrow. KK's heart soared, finding solace in Nisha's laughter, warmth in her care, and a companion in every challenge they faced. Every encounter felt like a new chapter, an exploration of the heart that KK had never dared to embark upon before.

Yet, despite their growing affection, the challenges of adolescence loomed ahead. Balancing schoolwork with budding romance was no small feat. They faced the pressure of exams, the looming specter of adulthood casting its shadow over their youthful exuberance. But through it all, KK learned that love can thrive even amidst chaos, and that shared laughter and understanding can illuminate even the darkest paths.

As the school year progressed, their friendship transformed into something deeper. They became a part of each other's lives, each day a testament to their unspoken promise to support one another. In the midst of homework, deadlines, and the pressures of teenage life, KK realized that love is not just found in grand gestures; sometimes, it's in the shared smiles over homework, in the stolen glances during class, and in the quiet moments when two hearts beat in perfect harmony.

With each passing day, their story unfolded a beautiful tapestry woven from the threads of friendship, love, and a determination to navigate the challenges ahead together. And so, in the heart of a middle-class boy, a love story began to bloom—fragile yet vibrant, innocent yet profound—forever changing the course of their lives.

* * * * *

Chapter 3

Price of Silence

Everything seemed to flow like a well-composed symphony as KK and Nisha moved into their 12th class. They navigated the maze of adolescence with laughter and shared dreams, their connection blossoming with every passing day. But as life often has a way of disrupting harmony, a new student named Sandeep entered their world, bringing chaos in his wake.

Sandeep was notorious—a brat whose reputation preceded him. He strolled into class with an air of bravado, casting a long shadow over the companionship that had flourished between KK and Nisha. He was known for his bad habits, including smoking and making crude comments about girls, a stark contrast to the innocence that KK and Nisha had cherished. While KK remained the quiet soul, Sandeep reveled in his notoriety, quickly making his presence felt.

As the first term examinations approached, tensions ran high. KK and Nisha were placed in separate rooms for the exams, but the real challenge lay in the presence of their accounts teacher, who had taken an unsettling interest in their relationship. During the examination, the teacher walked over to KK's desk, his voice dripping with disdain. "So, KK, how's your girlfriend? Heard she's quite popular these days," he sneered, his words like daggers aimed at Nisha's dignity.

KK felt a surge of protectiveness rise within him. How dare this man speak about Nisha in such a manner? "Please refrain from making such statements about her," KK shot back, his voice trembling with anger, but the teacher merely laughed, escalating the situation. As the comments became more derogatory, KK's patience wore thin. "I'll see you outside the school if you don't stop," he warned, fury burning in his heart.

The classroom fell silent, students wide-eyed, absorbing the intensity of the confrontation. The news spread like wildfire, reaching Nisha's ears, and though she was shocked by the ordeal, her heart swelled with gratitude. At that moment, she understood that KK felt as deeply for her as she did for him. Their bond strengthened, and for a while, they were wrapped in the warmth of mutual affection.

However, the arrival of Sandeep would soon shatter that fragile peace. Nisha was asked to sit with him, and distance began to subtly grow between KK and Nisha. At first, KK dismissed it, trusting Nisha wholeheartedly. But Sandeep's influence began to seep into her life. Nisha, concerned about Sandeep's smoking habits, approached KK, asking for his support in helping Sandeep quit.

"He just needs a friend, KK," she insisted, her compassion for others shining through.

Then Nisha extended her hand of friendship to Sandeep. What began as a noble endeavor soon took a turn that left KK reeling. The realization that Nisha had joined Sandeep for tuition at his home struck him like a thunderclap. "Why would you do that?" he asked with an edge of desperation in his voice. "You don't know him like I do," Nisha reassured him. "I'm just studying with him. You have to trust me."

KK forced a smile, his heart sinking as he watched Nisha grow closer to the boy who thrived on rebellion. Days turned into weeks, and it became painfully clear that Nisha was losing interest in their friendship. While KK worked hard to keep his grades up, Nisha's scores began to plummet. It hurt him to see her struggling, yet he held his tongue, believing love should never be a chain but a pair of wings.

Each day brought new heartache. Nisha would downplay her friendship with Sandeep during lunch breaks, assuring KK it was nothing serious. "He's just a friend, I promise," she'd say, but the words rang hollow. KK would listen, but the trust he once had began to shatter like glass, sharp and painful. He would watch her laugh with Sandeep, their connection deepening, while he felt like a ghost lingering in the shadows, yearning to reclaim what was once theirs.

I wore my heart like an open book,
But now its pages torn and shaken.
You chose a path I couldn't follow,
And now I face the weight of hollow.

One fateful day, Nisha approached KK with a look that broke his heart into a thousand pieces. "KK, I need to tell you something," she said, her voice barely above a whisper. "I've developed feelings for Sandeep." The words hung in the air like a heavy fog, suffocating him. The finality of her confession pierced through him, and the world around him blurred.

In a fit of anguish, they argued, their voices rising like a tempest. The distance that had formed between them now felt insurmountable. Every moment spent apart was a reminder of what they had lost. KK's heart ached to see the girl he adored drifting away, her laughter echoing with someone else. He had fought so hard to protect her dignity, only to lose her to the very person who had tarnished it.

As the school year continued, their communication dwindled. KK's concern for Nisha's declining grades remained a gnawing worry that settled in his heart like a stone. They no longer shared laughter or whispered secrets; the air between them thickened with unspoken words and broken promises. Despite the ache, KK chose to remain silent, believing that love could never be forced, even if it meant watching her slip away.

Though my heart cries out, I must stay mute,
For love unreciprocated bears no fruit.
I stand in the shadows, lost in despair,
While you chase your dreams, I'm gasping for air.

As the days turned into weeks, the farewell day for their class arrived. A bittersweet occasion where everyone celebrated their shared memories before parting ways to face the board exams. Joy mingled with sorrow as students received their titles, ready to take their next steps into the world. It was during this moment of reckoning that they found themselves face-to-face once again. "Good luck with your exams, KK," Nisha said, her voice trembling with unspoken emotions. "I'm really sorry for everything." KK forced a smile, masking the pain that threatened to consume him. "You always deserved something better, Nisha," he replied, his voice steady but his heart breaking. He wanted to scream, to tell her how much he still cared, but he held back, convinced that their paths would no longer intertwine.

As they exchanged farewell wishes, a quiet resolve settled over KK. He knew life had a way of weaving unexpected paths, but for now, he could only watch as the girl who had once captured his heart walked away, hand in hand with another. In that moment, he understood that love, while beautiful, could also be devastatingly fragile—a reminder of the delicate balance between trust and heartbreak.

After weeks of anticipation, the day of the board exam results arrived. The air was thick with anxiety as students gathered to check their scores. KK approached the notice board, heart pounding, and his mind racing with possibilities. As he scanned the list, relief washed over him—he had done reasonably well, earning grades that would open doors to further education. Yet, the joy was bittersweet.

Nisha's name appeared on the list, but the results were alarming. She had barely passed, her grades falling far short of what was needed for admission to a decent college. The weight of disappointment hung heavily in the air, and KK's heart sank for her. He could see the anguish etched across her face as she absorbed the reality of her situation.

"Where did we go wrong, Nisha?" he thought, unable to voice the sorrow swelling in his heart. The girl he had once known, vibrant and full of promise, was now staring into an uncertain future.

With a heavy heart, KK turned away, hoping that one day, perhaps in another life, their paths might cross again. And with that thought lingering in the air, he took a deep breath, preparing to face the storm that lay ahead, knowing that the echoes of their love would forever remain etched in his heart.

"When your first love fades, it leaves a scar in the form of a lesson, reminding you that even broken hearts keep beating– stronger than before."

* * * * *

Chapter 4

The Unwritten Curriculum of Love

As KK and his family scrambled across Delhi, visiting every college in sight, hearts racing against the cut-off lists and hopes tangled with every form they filled, he barely had time to breathe, let alone dream. The 99% walls seemed insurmountable, each cut-off line a reminder of his own limits. Then came an unexpected glimmer of hope: the college had an alternate route for admission, through sports trials. "Football," thought KK. His heart leaped. Football had always been a refuge, and now, it had turned into an opportunity. As he stood on the muddy field that day, waiting for his trial, his family's hopes felt like a weight on his shoulders. But as soon as he began to play, a sense of calm washed over him. It was more than just a game—it was his only chance. He gave it his all, and when he finally got his acceptance, a sense of relief and thrill rushed over him. KK was set to begin college. The journey wasn't what he'd expected, but it was the beginning of something new.

The night before his first day at college, KK tossed and turned, his mind spinning with both thrill and dread. He imagined walking through those gates, the smell of new books and the faint echoes of laughter and chatter filling the air. The fear of ragging by seniors haunted him, yet there was excitement for this new chapter that was starting. What would college be like? Would he find friends? But life seemed to favor him that day. As if by some stroke of fate, he quickly connected with two boys: Rohit and Yogesh.

Rohit, the son of a businessman, carried himself with confidence, while Yogesh had a fearless, carefree spirit. The three made an unlikely yet dynamic trio, a combination of daring, dreams, and quiet ambition. They were inseparable from the start, and that very first day, the three hatched a playful plan. They pretended to be seniors, throwing other freshers off guard with their 'senior' act, a harmless prank that left them feeling victorious. When the truth came out, their classmates gave them a title they wore proudly—the troublemakers. And thus began a bond as deep as brotherhood, each day an adventure in itself.

But the past has a way of reappearing at the least convenient times. As KK walked into the class one morning, laughing with his new-found friends, he froze. Nisha. She was there. The girl he'd thought he'd left behind. Memories of past misunderstandings and uncomfortable glances resurfaced, making his new life feel insecurely close to unraveling. KK's instinct was to avoid her, to erase the chance of confrontation or another awkward encounter. So, he decided to change his section, distancing himself from whatever turbulence her presence might bring. Rohit and Yogesh, ever loyal, made the switch with him.

With this new-found freedom, their days turned into a blur of laughter and carefree escapades. College wasn't about classes anymore; it was about exploring life beyond the confines of rules and routines. They spent their days in the canteen, lingering over endless cups of chai and watching life pass by with a blend of youthful hope and freedom. They talked about dreams, shared secrets, and lived without restraint, their lives becoming their own for the first time.

But as carefree as KK felt, life had more in store for him. He enrolled in a computer course in Noida—a decision less of choice and more of circumstance. Though he didn't feel any passion for computers, KK found himself adapting to a routine he hadn't imagined. College in the morning, the computer course in the evening, and a life woven in between.

And it was here, in the cramped, fluorescent-lit computer classroom, that he first saw her—Karuna. She had an effortless beauty, her presence radiant without trying, and an intelligence that spoke even in her silence. She sat at the front, focused and absorbed in every lesson, while KK, always at the back, found himself captivated by her every move. Watching her brought a calm he hadn't expected; it was a quiet enchantment that wrapped itself around him each day.

He'd watch her from afar, too shy to speak,
In a room filled with people, she was unique.
Her laugh was a song, her glance a dream,
In her world, his heart had found a theme.

Days turned into silent admiration until KK's heart could hold it no longer. The fear, the insecurity, the reminders of past rejections—it all faded in the gentle pull he felt toward her. One day, when she caught him looking, he quickly averted his gaze, feeling his cheeks burn. It was only a glance, but it was enough to set his heart racing.

Then came the day he knew he'd have to make his move. The monsoon rains had flooded the streets as his class ended. He saw her board a DTC bus, raindrops decorating her hair, and a sense of magic surrounding her. Compelled by something beyond words, he followed her. It was reckless, yes, but he couldn't hold back any longer.

They reached her stop, and he took a deep breath, calling her name softly as she stepped off. She turned, her eyes meeting his with a mixture of surprise and curiosity. Heart pounding, KK gathered his courage, his voice barely a whisper as he spoke the words he'd held back for too long.

"I love you," he began, his voice shaking yet earnest.
"I'd wait a lifetime for you if you'll let me."
Her silence was gentle, her smile kind,
As she asked for time, a request to unwind.

It wasn't a no, and that alone made his heart soar. That night, he lay awake, his mind a blur of dreams and hopes, the thought of her smile pulling him into a world where anything seemed possible. For the first time, he felt like the universe was on his side.

Days passed in a fog of anticipation, each moment a countdown to seeing her again. She remained distant, however, and KK's hope began to fade, replaced by the familiar ache of doubt. But he couldn't let go. After nearly a week, he gathered his courage once more. This time, as he asked for an answer, she looked at him, her gaze soft and unguarded, and simply nodded.

Her "yes" was a whisper that echoed for days,
A beacon of light, a golden haze.
In her words, he found a world anew,
A love as deep as morning dew.

KK felt as though he'd just conquered the world. For someone who had grown up with his own set of insecurities, and who had learned to limit his dreams, this moment was a victory beyond anything he could have imagined. In her, he'd found not just a dream but a whole universe, one that welcomed him with open arms.

For now, KK allowed himself to live fully in this new-found love, each day a silent promise, a bliss he'd never felt before.

* * * * *

Chapter 5

A Rose Forever

Love is a journey—one that often leads us through fields of roses and thorny paths alike. Each experience shapes us, teaches us, and sometimes breaks us. For KK, love was a bittersweet melody that began in the vibrant halls of his school and evolved into an emotional saga filled with beauty and pain.

They say love is a rose—
Beautiful and true,
But for every petal, there's a thorn,
Sharp, hidden, waiting to break through.

KK had found in Karuna something he'd never felt before—a pure, all-encompassing love that made each day worth waking up for. She was the light that filled his heart, the person he waited to see each afternoon. With every rose he gave her every day, he was handing her a piece of his soul, an unspoken promise to protect and cherish her forever. To him, she was like the delicate petals, and he wanted to be her thorn—her silent protector against anything that might harm her.

Their love story grew beyond the computer classes that first brought them together. They'd meet for lunches, and occasionally, he would surprise her with tickets to the latest movie. Every moment with her felt magical like he was living a fairy tale that no one else could understand. And whenever he looked into her eyes, he saw a future filled with warmth, understanding, and endless love. She was his reason to study hard, his muse, his dream, his reality. They exchanged scrapbooks filled with thoughts and confessions, each page more tender than the last.

Eyes like oceans, a heart so pure,
She was his strength, his world secure.
They wrote of dreams, of futures bright,
Together, they'd walk into the light.

But then, the dynamics shifted when Karuna opted for a women's college. It was during one of their conversations that she shared her fears, revealing that a guy had been following her whenever she left college. KK felt a surge of protectiveness wash over him. He couldn't let anyone intimidate her, and he knew he had to act. Determined to confront this boy, he rallied a couple of friends and set out to find the stalker.

In a fierce confrontation, KK faced the boy alone, fueled by anger and the need to protect Karuna. He beat the boy soundly, ensuring he wouldn't dare follow her again. The adrenaline coursed through him as he fought, each punch a testament to his love and loyalty. When he returned to Karuna, he found her looking at him with awe and gratitude, their bond deepening at that moment. She felt safe in his presence, and their friendship blossomed into something even more beautiful.

Then one day, without warning, she was gone. For three days, he watched the empty seat beside him in class, his heart growing heavier with each passing hour. He waited, hoping to catch a glimpse of her, but the class ended in silence, the rose in his hand beginning to wilt.

By the fourth day, his patience gave way to worry, and he decided to call her. He dialed her number, each ring amplifying his dread. Finally, her mother answered, her voice sharp and guarded.

"Is this the boy who has been giving her roses every day?" Her tone was cold, turning his excitement to unease.

"Yes," KK replied, his voice gentle but unwavering. "I am. I love her with all my heart, and I give her a rose every day because... because I want to marry her someday."

There was silence, heavy and damning. Then, her mother told him they wanted to meet. KK's heart raced as he agreed, anticipation and fear tangling within him. He waited for them at the computer institute, the rose in his hand trembling as much as his heart.

They arrived in an old Maruti 800, her mother stepping out first, her gaze fierce and filled with unspoken accusations. Her father sat in the car, watching from a distance. KK felt the weight of their judgment even before a word was spoken.

'Namaste,' he whispered, heart in hand,
But her mother's gaze was cold, unfeeling.
"How dare you dream? How dare you give—
Gifts you can't afford, a life you can't live?"

Her mother's words cut through him like shards of glass. She accused him of stealing, wasting his family's money on frivolous gestures, and leading her daughter astray. KK felt his heart breaking under the weight of her words, but he remained steady, answering only, "I love her. I want to be with her. Where is she?"

But they gave him no answers, no hint of understanding. Instead, her father stepped out of the car, calm but firm, instructing him to bring his own father the next day.

That evening, KK wrestled with the thoughts of how he would explain all of this to his father. He had never told him about Karuna, never shared this secret part of his life with the man he respected most. But he knew he had no choice. After dinner, he mustered all the courage he had and told his father everything—about the roses, the love, the promises he had made to Karuna. His father's reaction was a mixture of anger and disbelief. But after a moment's silence, he agreed to meet her family.

In that quiet night, he dared to dream,
Of futures bright, of a love supreme.
He saw himself beside his bride,
And in that vision, their worlds collide.

The night was filled with restless anticipation. He lay awake, imagining every possibility, every way the meeting might go. He could already see their families coming together, his parents accepting Karuna as his life partner, her parents seeing the depth of his love, understanding that his intentions were pure. He clung to these thoughts, his heart alight with hope.

But when morning came, the lightness he'd felt dissolved with the rising sun. As he and his father arrived at the institute, KK's heart sank at the sight of Karuna's parents, their expressions unreadable and closed.

Her father stepped forward first, addressing KK's father with a calm but pointed tone. They spoke of family expectations, values, and priorities. They didn't ask KK any questions; they didn't care about his feelings, his dreams, or the promises he'd made. To them, he was simply a boy from an ordinary family with no right to pursue a love as lofty as this.

His father listened, trying to defend KK, but each word fell heavily in the silence that lingered. And then her mother spoke the final words that shattered him: "Our daughter has gone to stay with her relatives. She will not be returning. She will not be seeing you again."

KK felt his world collapse. He looked at his father and her parents, desperately trying to find a reason, a way to fix what had gone so wrong. But the doors had closed. The rose he held, once full of promise, seemed to wither in his hands.

One last petal, one last tear,
One last hope lost to fear.
In that moment, a dream died quickly,
Love's flame quenched, its light surpassed.

Days turned into weeks, and the space beside him in class remained empty. Every rose he'd ever given her felt like a reminder of what could have been. The memories they'd shared, the promises they'd whispered to each other, haunted him like an unfulfilled melody that lingered long after the music had stopped.

When love fades like the morning mist,
And memories become a painful twist,
The heart aches in silent screams,
Longing for lost, unfulfilled dreams.

Later, after a week, she rejoined her classes deliberately ignoring KK. He began to withdraw. Class held no meaning for him anymore. The lessons that once felt vibrant with her beside him turned hollow, like echoes of a world that no longer existed. KK found himself wandering, lost in his own grief, bunking classes because it was easier than facing her indifference. Each day, he'd still show up, hoping she might change her mind, hoping she'd look at him the way she used to. But she never did.

Her birthday arrived – a day he had always celebrated with her, a day he'd thought about for weeks in advance. Determined to show her how much he still cared, he arranged a surprise with their mutual friends. He ordered a cake, decorated it with roses, and ensured that she'd be the first to taste it. Through a friend, he made sure she received the first slice. But the moment passed in silence. She ate the cake, gave a polite nod, and walked away, her eyes as blank as ever. It was as though he had become invisible.

The celebration he'd poured his heart into went unnoticed. She didn't spare him even a second's glance. KK watched as she drifted away, each step deepening the ache in his heart, the emptiness gnawing at him. He realized that all his efforts to win her back were slipping away, unnoticed, unappreciated, as though his love had been erased from her memory.

Hope became a weary ghost,
A shadow in a love once close.
She turned away, he fell apart,
With empty hands and a broken heart.

The pain began to show in other parts of his life. KK, who had once been so full of promise, flunked his first year of B.Com (H), his mind too clouded by heartache to focus on his studies. He decided to switch to B.Com (P), realizing that even his academic dreams seemed hollow without her by his side. In the two years that followed, he struggled, pouring his energy into his coursework, yet never shaking off the emptiness her absence had left. She was everywhere and nowhere, haunting his thoughts with memories of what had once been.

The day finally arrived—the last day of his computer course. KK knew it was his last chance to say goodbye, to find closure. He rehearsed what he'd say, words of farewell that carried both gratitude and the sadness he'd held onto all this time. But as he approached her, she turned her back, walking away without a glance, leaving him standing there, words unsaid and heart abandoned. It was over. He had to accept it now—she was gone, and there would be no second chance, no miracle.

In love's remains, a whispered plea,
For what was lost, what could not be?
As petals fell and roses died,
He watched his love drift with the tide.

Three years of his life, three years of hopes, dreams, and memories—all now reduced to ashes. She had become nothing more than a fading memory, an ache in his heart, a rose that had bloomed once but now lay forgotten, withered by time and neglect. KK left the institute that day, not just saying goodbye to her but to a part of himself—the young, hopeful dreamer who had believed in love's power to conquer anything.

Yet, in the quiet that followed, he realized he had no choice but to move on. He would build a life for himself, and find purpose beyond the love that had left him so broken. With a heavy heart and a steely resolve, he stepped out into the world, knowing that life, somehow, would go on.

The rose was gone, the thorn remained,
A love that left but still sustained.
And as he walked, he knew at last,
The pain of love's unyielding past.

In time, the ache of loss morphed into a quiet strength. He still remembered the roses, the laughter, and the love that had once filled his heart, but he also learned to appreciate the journey he had undertaken. Love had been a beautiful, painful teacher, and in its wake, it had crafted a new version of him—stronger, wiser, and more resilient. KK learned then that love, no matter how pure, sometimes falls victim to forces beyond control. He would carry the memory of Karuna, the girl who taught him the beauty and cruelty of love, for the rest of his life. And with that, he became the thorn—protecting his own heart, guarding it from ever being hurt so deeply again.

The love he had once known became a gentle whisper in the background, guiding him, reminding him of the beauty of life and the possibilities that still lay ahead. He had weathered the storm and emerged transformed, ready to embrace whatever came next. But even in the years that followed, he never forgot the girl who had been his rose and the love that had once made his world bloom.

"They all told me time would heal, but how do you heal when the wound looks at you with your ex's eyes every day?"

* * * * *

Chapter 6

A Symphony of Resilience

In the stillness of his thoughts, KK grappled with the aftermath of Karuna's rejection. He had begun to believe that no heart, except his mother's, could truly love him for who he was. Life felt unbearably heavy, a burden he couldn't share with his family. They depended on him, and revealing his pain was not an option. Instead, he donned a mask of determination, concealing his heartache behind a facade of unwavering resolve.

As he completed his graduation, KK was filled with determination to secure a job without delay. The thought of idling away even a single day was unbearable. With unwavering focus, he set out to explore every possible opportunity, leaving no stone unturned in his pursuit.

Day after day, he hustled, pouring all his energy into applications, interviews, and networking. The journey was far from easy, but KK's resilience never wavered. Then, one morning, just as the sun peeked through his window, his phone buzzed with an email.

It was an offer to work at a publication house. The words on the screen blurred for a moment as he blinked, trying to grasp the reality of what he was seeing. This was the break he had been waiting for, the first step toward building the life he had always envisioned.

He immersed himself in his work, channeling every ounce of energy into building a brighter future for himself and his family. With each keystroke, he hoped to mend the pieces of his heart that lay scattered in the wake of rejection. He envisioned a life where he could elevate his family's living standards, vowing that no girl would ever have the power to turn him away again.

The opportunity of a lifetime arrived unexpectedly when, just a month into his new job, he received a call from a prestigious IT company, offering him a decent salary and a five-day work week. Overjoyed, KK felt a flicker of happiness ignite within him. While love may have eluded him, his career was beginning to flourish, filling the void left by his unfulfilled heart.

Driven by a renewed sense of ambition and an insatiable desire to learn more, KK enrolled in a two-year master's program in Commerce, managing his classes on Saturdays while balancing his job. On the first day of class, he scanned the bulletin board, seeking his name and class when he met Vikrant Sharma, a fellow student who would soon become his closest friend. Their connection was sudden; they bonded over shared dreams, aspirations, and a mutual determination to succeed.

As the semester progressed, their eyes were drawn to two enchanting girls in their class—Meher and Vandana.

Both possessed an allure that was impossible to resist. KK felt a magnetic pull toward Meher, but when he discovered her religion, doubt clouded his heart. Nevertheless, her grace and charm captivated him, igniting a passion he couldn't contain. Vikrant felt a similar connection with Vandana, and soon, the four of them formed a vibrant circle of friendship, brimming with laughter, study sessions, and camaraderie.

With their friendship blossoming, Vikrant and KK devised a plan to approach Meher and Vandana. They decided to sit behind the girls during class, gradually becoming the center of attention for their academic diligence. Their commitment to submitting assignments on time caught the eye of their classmates, and they proudly declared Meher and Vandana as their 'babies'.

KK devoted himself to Meher in every way possible—completing her assignments, assisting her with her studies, and cherishing every moment they spent together. The feelings he harbored for her deepened with each passing day, and as the semester approached its end, he knew it was time to confess his love.

On a serene Saturday afternoon, bathed in sunlight, KK and Vikrant took their loved ones out to celebrate. Vikrant, feeling heartened, led Vandana to a quiet corner of the café, where excitement mingled with nerves.

"Vandana," he began, his voice steady yet warm, "these past months have been incredible, and I can't imagine a future without you. I want to support your dreams and share every moment together. Will you be my girlfriend?"

Vandana's eyes sparkled with surprise as her smile blossomed. "Oh, Vikrant! I've been waiting for this moment. Yes, I'd love to be your girlfriend!" Their hands intertwined, forging a bond that felt destined.

Meanwhile, KK found himself alone with Meher, the weight of unspoken words pressing heavily on his heart. "Meher," he began, his voice trembling, "you mean the world to me. You brighten my life, and I've fallen for you deeply. Will you embark on this journey with me?"

Meher's expression shifted, a flicker of sadness clouding her beautiful eyes. "KK, I care about you profoundly. You're an amazing person, but we belong to different religions. My family wouldn't accept this, and I can't bear the thought of you being hurt if things don't work out. I promise to be your best friend until the end."

The words struck him like a dagger. KK felt as if the ground had shifted beneath him, his heart splintering into countless pieces. "But Meher, I'm willing to fight for us," he pleaded, desperation lacing his voice. "I can show you that love knows no religion."

Tears filled her eyes, but she shook her head gently. "You deserve someone who can fully commit to you without hesitation. Please understand that I want you in my life, just not as something more than friends."

With his heart aching, KK silently vowed to make her fall in love with him, despite the uncertainty that lay ahead. He refused to accept defeat, for a flicker of hope still burned within him.

In the silence, a promise was made,
A heart still beating, though heavy with shadow.
He whispered softly, as shadows loomed near,
"One day, dear Meher, I'll show you I'm here."

As the first year of their master's program came to a close, the four friends united once more, their bond unbreakable. They established a ritual of sitting together during exams, sharing notes, and encouraging one another. With Vikrant and Vandana's relationship blossoming, their companionship flourished, and they playfully encouraged Meher to recognize KK's devotion.

The atmosphere during their exams was thick with tension, but KK felt a sense of peace knowing Meher was by his side, even if their relationship remained unfulfilled. They exchanged glances and shared jokes to lighten the mood, their friendship transcending the pressures of academic life.

As they completed their exams, stepping out together, the laughter and light-heartedness returned, showcasing the strength of their bond. Vikrant's ongoing nudges for Meher to accept KK's love added a layer of humor to their situation, brightening the anxiety-filled environment.

After finishing the first year with nearly equal scores, their friendship grew even deeper, intertwining their lives with rich experiences and cherished memories. Yet as the second year loomed on the horizon, KK was acutely aware of the challenges that awaited.

Yet in the depths of my silent plea,
I'll weave my dreams, you'll come to see,
That love can conquer, it knows no chain,
And through the darkness, I'll break this pain.

As they celebrated the completion of their first year, laughter and joy filled the air, but the weight of unspoken emotions lingered between KK and Meher. Each shared moment felt bittersweet, and as KK gazed at her, he resolved to show her the depths of his heart—no matter the challenges that lay ahead.

As the sun dipped below the horizon, casting long shadows on their path, KK felt the warmth of hope surge within him. He wouldn't give up; he would demonstrate that love, in all its complexities, was worth fighting for. The journey was just beginning, and KK was ready to chase his dreams, his heart forever anchored to Meher, the girl who held his heart captive.

* * * * *

Chapter 7

A Story Unfinished

As the second year of their master's program began, the bonds of friendship between KK, Vikrant, Vandana, and Meher flourished like a vibrant garden in full bloom. Each day felt like a new adventure, filled with laughter, shared secrets, and the thrill of youthful discovery. They were inseparable—a quartet of hearts that danced to the rhythm of college life, where every moment was stitched into the fabric of their memories.

In laughter's echo, we carved our names,
In corridors bustling with hopes and dreams.
With coffee and whispers, we played our games,
Woven together in life's flowing streams.

The campus buzzed with excitement as they traversed its paths, the sun casting a golden hue on their aspirations. Countless afternoons were spent in the dimly lit corners of the library, surrounded by the rustle of pages and the murmur of knowledge being shared. They were a familiar sight at local cafés, huddled around steaming cups of coffee, the air thick with camaraderie and the scent of pastries. Movies became their escape, where they would lose themselves in tales of love and friendship, laughter echoing in darkened theaters like an anthem of their youth. Each moment was a thread woven into the rich tapestry of their shared experiences—a collective memory that would forever hold a special place in their hearts.

Assignments became their lifeline, a shared responsibility that further tightened their bond. They gathered in one of their homes, spread out textbooks and notes, exchanging ideas and scribbling down solutions. Late-night study sessions turned into heartfelt discussions where dreams and fears intertwined, the lines between friendship and something deeper beginning to blur. It was during these times that KK felt most alive—his dedication to Meher fueled his ambition, and he found himself excelling in both his academic and professional life.

In study halls, where silence spoke,
We shared our dreams, the unbroken hope.
In every glance, a spark ignites,
As love whispered softly in the nights.

At work, KK's commitment earned him recognition, leading him to collaborate directly with the CIO on crucial projects. His confidence soared, allowing him to bring fresh ideas to the table. Yet, despite his professional success, his heart remained tethered to Meher, and every shared smile or fleeting touch ignited hope within him. "What is this feeling," he often mused in the quiet moments, "if not love as she became his mobile wallpaper?"

Then came Aastha, a witty and spirited girl who seamlessly integrated into their group, her laughter a refreshing breeze amidst the storm of their emotions. She brought a new energy, her playful banter igniting a fire of mischief. With her knack for creating tension, Aastha often stirred the pot, teasing KK and Meher while observing the subtle shifts in their dynamics. Her presence added a layer of complexity to their friendship; she reveled in the chaos of emotions, her antics both light-hearted and infuriating.

One day, as Meher ran late for class, Aastha seized an opportunity for mischief. "Let's chat," she suggested, leading KK to an empty classroom with a mischievous grin. Under the guise of casual conversation, Aastha leaned in, her intent masked by a playful demeanor, testing the boundaries of their friendship with a bold kiss. Just as the world tilted beneath them, Meher burst through the door, her eyes wide with disbelief.

"KK!" she shouted, pushing Aastha aside and delivering a stinging slap to his face. The sound echoed in the silence, a moment frozen in time. Meher's tears fell freely as she stormed out, leaving KK paralyzed with shock and a confusing sense of joy. Did her reaction mean she loved? The realization sent his heart racing, a tumult of emotions battling within.

Though he rushed after her, calling her name, Meher had vanished, her heart heavy with betrayal. The following days were unbearable; KK's attempts to reach her were met with silence. He pleaded with Vikrant and Vandana, but

Meher refused to listen. She was drowning in her emotions, the distance between them growing unbearable.

Tears like rain, in silence fell,
A heart divided, a pain to quell.
In shadows lingered love unspoken,
With every moment, another bond is broken.

As the sun dipped below the horizon, casting a warm glow over the campus, Meher returned to college one fateful Saturday; her resolve was still fragile. KK, desperate to make amends, dropped to his knees in front of their classmates, holding his ears in a traditional gesture of apology. "I'm sorry for hurting you, Meher. Please forgive me," he pleaded. The sight of him vulnerable melted Meher's heart. She rushed to him, pulling him away from the curious stares of their peers, dragging him to the canteen where she poured out her heart.

"How dare you allow her to kiss you?" she demanded, her voice cracking with hurt. "I can't stand Aastha!"

As she unleashed her fury, KK stood quietly, absorbing her pain, his heart aching with every word. When she finally finished, he smiled softly, a warmth blooming within him. "And you still say you don't love me?"

Meher's anger dissipated, replaced by a flicker of affection as she admitted, "I can't tolerate you being with anyone else." At that moment, KK knew he had broken through her defenses; love had, perhaps, taken root within her heart.

As their days together unfolded, Meher became possessive of KK, intertwining their lives further. They walked hand in hand through the corridors, marking their territory to others. Each shared glance ignited an unspoken understanding; their friendship had blossomed into something beautiful yet tumultuous.

In every touch, a fire burned brightly,
In whispers exchanged, love took flight.
Yet shadows danced in the corners of dreams,
As reality tugged at the seams.

But the storm clouds loomed over Meher's life. A property dispute within her family sent ripples of distress through her home, leaving her unprepared for the upcoming exams. When she confided in Vikrant and Vandana, they tried to reassure her, but KK's resolve was unwavering.

"I won't sit for the exam if you don't," he declared, his heart racing. "I love you, Meher. I can't leave you behind."

"Are you nuts?" she shouted, her frustration spilling over. "Why would you ruin your future for me?"

"Because you matter," he replied firmly, refusing to back down. "Trust me; let's make this work."

Meher, overwhelmed yet trusting, reluctantly agreed to sit for the exam, with KK's encouragement ringing in her ears. "Just sit to my right," he instructed, and she nodded, still hesitant, but the warmth of his words gave her the courage she needed.

The day of the exam arrived, and KK took off from his work, pouring every ounce of energy into preparation. The tension outside the exam hall was palpable as classmates gathered, but KK's focus was solely on Meher, waiting for her arrival. When she finally burst through the door, her smile was a beacon of hope.

"Why haven't you gone inside?" she asked, breathless with excitement.

"Because I was waiting for you," he replied, taking her hand as they rushed inside, their fingers entwined as if they were the only two souls in a crowded room.

Seated beside one another, the weight of the world faded as the exam began. Meher looked at KK, confusion etched on her face as she realized she had no answers. Panic flickered in her eyes, and KK felt a knot tighten in his heart. He motioned for her to pretend to write, his heart racing as he plotted his next move. When the invigilator turned her back, KK quickly swapped papers, scribbling furiously to fill Meher's answer sheet, his hand moving like a man possessed.

Tears glistened in Meher's eyes as she watched him write, overwhelmed by the depth of his love. "Why do you love me so much when you know you can't have me?" she whispered as they exchanged papers once more.

"Because my heart doesn't care about what's possible," he answered simply, his eyes filled with determination.

With every exam, KK took the same chance to ensure Meher succeeded, pouring his heart into her answers as if they were his own. The day they finished, there was an air of bittersweet finality. Meher's embrace lingered longer than usual, tears flowing freely as they hugged goodbye, a moment suspended in time.

In every tear, a story was spun,
Of love unreturned, yet brightly begun.
Though paths may twist and time may part,
Forever you'll linger within my heart.

"I can't say I love you," she confessed, her voice trembling, "but you will always be someone I cherish until my last breath."

As they pulled away, KK's heart raced, a flurry of emotions swirling within him. He felt the weight of unfulfilled desire, the ache of longing etched into his very soul. They stood in silence, the world around them fading, their unspoken words hanging heavy in the air.

As they parted ways, KK knew that sometimes love is about letting go and cherishing the memories that would linger. His heart ached with the knowledge that their paths would diverge, yet the imprint of Meher would remain, a melody playing softly in the background of his life.

In the weeks that followed, the distance grew palpable. Meher moved on, her family arranging her marriage in haste, a fate that KK would never understand.

When results day arrived, KK, Vikrant, and Vandana rushed to college, hopeful that Meher would join them. But she stayed hidden, nervous about facing KK. When they finally met, he consoled her, saying, "It's okay. You were never mine to lose."

As they checked the results, the air was thick with anticipation. Meher's joy radiated through the room as she discovered she had passed, her eyes bright with happiness. But the reality hit hard—KK had scored just a little higher.

Tears welled in her eyes as she hugged him tightly. "I'm so sorry for everything," she whispered, her voice trembling.

KK held her close, knowing this was their moment—a bittersweet farewell. In that embrace, they held the essence of their love, a silent promise that would linger long after they parted.

In every heartbeat, our love shall remain,
A secret whispered, a soft refrain.
Though fate may lead us on separate ways,
In memories cherished, our hearts will blaze.

As they stepped away, KK watched her leave, the ache of unfulfilled dreams pulling at his heart. In the silence, he understood that true love is often unclaimed, a bittersweet blessing that shapes our lives. Meher would always be a part of him, a melody that echoed through the corridors of his heart.

And so, he stood at the crossroads of his life, silently grieving the love that could never be, knowing that in the depths of his heart, Meher would always linger, a soft reminder of the beauty and pain of love unspoken.

"Her goodbye wasn't just the end of a chapter; it was the closing of a book I wasn't ready to stop writing, leaving my heart as an unfinished story."

* * * * *

Chapter 8

The Blush of Love, The Ache of Guilt

By now, KK had nearly abandoned hope in love. He had tried, over and over, but life seemed to have other plans. Love came and went, each time leaving a deeper scar, and now, he was starting to believe that the universe had set him aside, saving love for others. His heart, worn and weary, could still ache for it, but he no longer believed it could ever be his.

And so, in the quiet of his solitude, he turned to poetry, pouring his sadness onto pages that no one knew he carried. He adopted the pen name Gum, which meant sadness, and under his blog *Gum Ki Kalam Se*, he laid bare his pain for strangers who somehow understood. His poetry spoke of longing, betrayal, and the aching beauty of dreams lost too soon. His verses found an audience as if his sorrow resonated with souls far and wide. In those lines, he discovered a strange peace—a small comfort in sharing his burden with the world.

The heart had surrendered to love's every shade,
Every time a hand slipped away, only memories remained.

His heart, though exhausted, still held fragments of warmth, pieces he didn't know how to offer anymore. But in his life, he still had some sources of light. At work, he met two friends who changed his days for the better—Deepankur and Senthil. With Deepankur's infectious laughter and dreamer's spirit and Senthil's gentle warmth, the three of them became like brothers. Their friendship gave KK a sense of belonging he'd almost forgotten. Nights were filled with laughter and long drives, conversations that wandered from dreams to regrets, and the joyful feeling that, perhaps, he didn't have to be alone.

Their friendship became his anchor, pulling him from the weight of his past. Deepankur, always bubbling with business ideas, was a Punjabi with a carefree charm. Senthil, who had fallen deeply for a girl who demanded he 'make something' of himself, added a balance to the trio's dynamic. Together, they planned outings, weekend getaways, and countless nights of laughter. They were a family in the truest sense, sharing not just time but the rarest of bonds—trust.

True friends are the roots beneath our tree,
Silent, steadfast, setting us free.
Through storms and calm, they never part,
A whispered prayer, a piece of heart.

Yet, even amidst this joy, KK's despair still lingered like a shadow. One night, after a celebratory dinner, they were driving back when two local bikers swerved close to Deepankur's car, ramming the bumper. They started taunting the trio with vulgar insults, calling them names too obscene to repeat. KK clenched his fists, trying to ignore it. But the taunts grew louder, the language uglier, until KK couldn't hold back. The bikers mocked their families, their mothers and sisters, and something deep within him snapped. Without thinking, he jumped out of the car, grabbing the handbrake lock. Senthil tried to hold him back, but KK was already in a fury, confronting the bikers.

In those brief minutes, KK poured out all the anger he'd held inside for years, each blow a release of frustration and heartbreak. The biker's friend ran, and KK's fury focused solely on the remaining man. Deepankur and Senthil rushed to stop him, finally pulling him back when they saw his bleeding hand, with glass shards cutting deep into his wrist. Their panic turned to urgency as they wrapped his wound with a towel and sped to the hospital. KK, lost in his rage, hadn't even noticed the blood pooling out of his wrists.

As they waited in the hospital, with Senthil holding a towel to KK's hand, they laughed about the fight, masking their worry. Deepankur looked at KK, his voice soft. "*Yaar, hum toh bas saath hain, hamesha,*" he said. KK felt a swell of gratitude for his friends, for these brothers who would stay by his side no matter how messy life became.

But even with such cherished friendships, KK's nights remained heavy. He turned back to his poetry, *Gum Ki Kalam Se*, crafting verses that grew sadder and deeper like pieces of his soul spread across a canvas for strangers to witness.

One evening, as he browsed his blog's comments, he noticed a familiar name—Swati—a fellow poet who regularly left him words of encouragement. She had a blog called SMS and her verses spoke of heartbreak, lost love, and dreams that faded with time. Her words felt like mirrors to his own pain, and over time, they began exchanging comments, each one revealing glimpses of themselves. Swati was from Indore, the daughter of a colonel, and a physiotherapist. Her life held its own burdens and its own scars, and slowly, KK found himself drawn to her.

Their online connection became late-night conversations, with calls that stretched till dawn. In her voice, he found comfort, a soothing balm to his wounded heart. She encouraged his poetry and admired his thoughts, and somewhere in her presence, KK began to feel whole again. Swati became a part of his world, not by asking, but by simply being there, accepting every part of him without judgment.

She was a stranger, yet felt like mine,
Her words spoke of feelings I'd left behind.
In her voice, I found a familiar tone,
A connection so deep, it felt like home.

Days turned into weeks, and KK knew his heart was slipping—falling for her in ways he hadn't expected. He had learned to guard his emotions, to hide them behind sarcasm and cleverness, but with Swati, something felt different. It was as if she was unlocking a door he had long kept closed.

One night, as they were chatting, with trembling words, he finally said, "I love you." His heart raced, half-expecting rejection and to be hurt again. But to his surprise, Swati didn't pull away. Instead, she opened up and shared stories of her own past, her own heartbreak. She revealed that she had been in a long-term relationship, that had grown stale, with a partner who had always seemed too distant, too indifferent. She spoke of the pain of unspoken words and the quiet distance that had torn apart something she once thought would last forever.

In their late-night conversations, they spoke of everything—nothing was too small, too mundane. She told him that she was pursuing a Bachelor of Physiotherapy (BPT) in Indore, which would soon be over, and then she would start looking for a job. KK, in turn, shared that he was working with a renowned IT company, thriving in his career while hiding the scars of his past.

Their conversations grew more personal as they began discussing the simplest things—the clothes they wore, the meals they ate, and the little moments that colored their days. Swati would often laugh, describing the comfort of wearing her favorite oversized sweater while sipping tea, and KK would smile, telling her about his mundane office meetings and how he longed for moments like these with her.

Despite the physical distance, their bond deepened with every word, every laugh, and every shared silence. They found solace in each other's company, the distance between them shrinking with each conversation. It was a connection that KK had never anticipated and one that left him wondering if maybe, just maybe, he could find the love he had long given up on.

And then, one day, unexpectedly, she was in Delhi. She called him, saying she was at Dilli Haat with her mother, and invited him to meet her in person. KK felt both excitement and creeping anxiety; he had never felt her before. They had shared words, hearts, and secrets, but not faces. Borrowing money from Deepankur and Senthil, he took an auto to Dilli Haat, his nerves prickling with anticipation. But when he saw her, his heart sank.

Swati wasn't the beautiful face he had conjured in his mind. She had a strong, plain face, her nose a bit larger than he'd imagined. For a brief, shameful moment, he thought of leaving, of turning away before she noticed him. But then, something held him back. Her face was plain, but her eyes—her eyes held kindness, warmth, an understanding that melted his hesitation.

They spoke awkwardly at first, and then with growing ease. She introduced him to her mother, who greeted him with warmth, and despite his initial discomfort, he found himself smiling, laughing even. As they bid goodbye, he felt a strange sense of guilt mingled with relief. But later that night, his phone began to ring. It was Swati, calling him over and over, her name lighting up his screen.

But KK, caught in his own self-doubt and disappointment, could not bring himself to pick up. The coldness in his heart grew as Swati's calls continued, one after another, a reminder of the rejection he had already started to feel. He kept his phone on silent and turned into stone. Every time the phone rang, it felt like a weight on his heart, but he turned his back on it. It was as if he couldn't bear to face the truth—that in the end, he wasn't sure if he wanted her. She was everything he needed, and yet, in that moment, she felt like another person he could disappoint, another love that could escape him.

As the calls grew, KK only sank deeper into his retreat. He reached home late, his body drained and his mind unsettled. He threw his phone on the sofa and collapsed into bed, not bothering to check the missed calls, not even acknowledging the persistent ringing in the background. He closed his eyes, hoping to forget everything, even her. He fell asleep in a haze of confusion and guilt.

The next morning, the light seemed harsher than usual, the room too bright, too real. KK awoke with a heaviness in his heart and a dull throb in his head. He reached for his phone, hoping for a few moments of peace before the day began. As he unlocked it, his eyes widened. There were around 200 missed calls from Swati.

For a moment, time seemed to freeze. His mind raced, trying to process the weight of what he had done. He felt guilt flood through him as if her repeated attempts to reach him were an accusation. He thought back to the night before—how he had turned her away, how he had shut her out simply because he was afraid. Afraid that love would slip away again. Afraid that this, too, was just another fleeting moment, a cruel joke played by destiny.

The guilt ate at him until he couldn't bear it anymore. KK's fingers trembled as he dialed her number. His heart pounded in his chest as he waited for her to pick up. But when the call connected, it wasn't the voice of someone angry or upset. Instead, there was a softness in Swati's voice. Her voice soft, replied, "KK, I know you didn't find me beautiful." Her words were a balm to his fractured soul. It was like the weight of everything he had feared was suddenly lifted, replaced by an unexpected warmth. Swati, the girl he had almost rejected, was here, still standing by him, still waiting for him to realize that he was worth loving. She didn't judge him, didn't question him. Instead, she forgave him. And in that moment, KK felt his heart crack open, finally understanding what true love might look like.

At that moment, KK realized the true meaning of love—not perfection, not idealized images, but acceptance. The kind of love that forgave, understood the scars and still chose to stay.

Not perfect by the world's design,
But in his flaws, her heart did find,
A love that's real, not bound by sight,
She saw his soul, and that felt right.

KK's heart was pounding as he whispered, "Swati, I love you. I want to marry you."

She paused, and then, in her gentle voice, replied, "Let's take it slow, KK. But I know you are worth it," as she headed back to Indore.

For the first time in years, he felt hope—a fragile, trembling hope that maybe, just maybe, love was still possible...

* * * * *

Chapter 9

Love's Reckoning

KK sat in his office, the hum of the fluorescent lights above almost drowned out by the constant buzzing of his phone. His work was a blur, his mind wrapped up in one thought—Swati. His heart, once locked away in a cold, cynical cage, had begun to thaw in ways he hadn't expected. Her laughter. Her voice. The way she understood him was like no one else had. And yet, he had hurt her. He had let his emotions slip; he had spoken too quickly and too rashly. The guilt weighed on him like a ton of bricks.

He sat at his desk, glancing at his phone every few seconds, hoping, praying that it would ring, that a message would pop up. But no, the screen remained stubbornly blank.

Then, like a miracle, it happened. At around 11:00 am, the phone buzzed in his hand. Sona, the name he had lovingly chosen for her, appeared on the screen.

His heart skipped a beat. He nearly dropped the phone in his haste to answer it. "Hello?" His voice was shaky, a mix of nerves and anticipation.

"Hey KK," Swati's voice floated through, warm and soft, like a comforting breeze. "I know things were a little tense earlier, and I'm really sorry. I just needed some time to sort through my feelings. I've been thinking about you, about us."

His breath caught in his throat. She called. She was talking to him.

"No, no," he quickly interjected, his words tumbling out. "You have nothing to apologize for. I've been a fool. I hurt you, and I'm so sorry." Swati's voice was gentle but firm. "KK, you didn't hurt me on purpose.

The weight on KK's heart lifted instantly. The relief flooded over him like a wave, leaving behind a warm, fluttering feeling he couldn't describe. He found himself smiling without realizing it.

"I've been waiting for you to call," he admitted, his voice soft and vulnerable. "I didn't know how to fix things without talking to you."

And just like that, his heart felt lighter. The weight that had crushed him for days seemed to dissolve, replaced with a warm, fluttering feeling he couldn't quite name. He could feel the smile tugging at his lips.

They spoke for an hour about her road trip, the places she had visited, and the exhaustion weighing on her. She mentioned needing to rest for a bit, but before hanging up, KK hesitated. There was something he had to say—something important.

"Swati, before you go, there's something I need to ask you," he said, his voice quiet but urgent. "But before that, I need to tell you about my past. I need you to understand who I am and where I come from."

Swati, ever patient, replied softly, "I'm listening."

As the day dragged on, every minute seemed to stretch longer. KK's mind raced as he looked at the clock again and again. His stomach was in knots, a mixture of excitement and fear about the night ahead. He wondered what she would say, what she might feel when she heard the truth. Would she accept it? Would she understand? Would she still want him?

The hours crept by.

Finally, at 8:00 pm, when KK was halfway through his dinner, his phone buzzed again, this time with a message from Swati.

"Up for a call?"

His heart did a flip. He looked at the clock, his pulse quickening. This was it. This was the moment. He quickly typed back, his fingers trembling. "Always for you."

He rushed to his room, locking the door behind him for privacy, and dialed her number. As the phone rang, he could feel his heart in his throat. Would she pick it up? Would she be mad? Would she still care?

"Hello," Swati's voice came through, soft and sweet.

"Sona," he said, a rush of emotion filling him. "I missed you."

There was a playful silence on the other end before Swati's laughter filled the space between them. "Well, that's how it should be," she teased. "Keep missing me, KK."

The sound of her laugh—the same laugh that had once made his heart ache with longing—was now like music to his ears. It made him feel safe and wanted like he was home.

They exchanged stories about their day, and KK found himself laughing at her jokes, smiling at the way she described the food she ate on her trip and the sights she saw. It was as if the distance between them had dissolved, and they were back in the familiar rhythm of their conversations. But then, the mood shifted. KK could no longer hold back.

"Swati," he said, his voice low and serious, "I need to know something. Do you love me?"

For a brief moment, there was only silence. His heart thudded in his chest, his breath shallow. What would she say?

But then, Swati's voice came softly. "I like you, KK," she said, her words slow and careful. "But I need time to think. I've been hurt before, and I don't want to rush into anything."

KK felt a sharp pang in his heart. It was a blow, but he nodded in understanding.

"I get it," he said, his voice soft. "I really do. Take all the time you need."

But something inside him refused to let it end there. He needed her to know the truth.

"Before you make any decision," he said with his voice filled with raw honesty, "I want you to know everything about me. I've been through a lot, Swati. I've loved Nisha, Karuna, and Meher before. I thought I knew what love was. But I was wrong. None of them were the one. They weren't the truth. But you... you're different. I've never felt this way about anyone before."

Swati listened quietly, her silence almost unbearable to KK. But when he finished, she spoke with a soft laugh. "I never knew you were a playboy," she teased.

KK chuckled nervously. "No, I wasn't. I was just looking for something real. Something lasting."

"But you've fallen in love with so many girls," Swati remarked with a smile in her voice.

"I know," KK said, his voice quiet, almost guilty. "But each time, I thought I had found it. I thought I had found the one, but it wasn't right. I wasn't ready until you."

Swati's laughter filled his ears once more. "You really are something, KK," she said with affection and warmth in her words. "But... do you love me?"

KK's heart pounded in his chest. He had said it to others before, but never like this. This was different.

"I do, Swati," he said, the words slipping out before he could stop them. "I love you. I want to be with you. I want to be your future."

For a long moment, Swati didn't respond. Then she said, "I need time. But I like you too. I really do."

KK smiled, his heart aching with longing. "Take all the time you need. I'll be here, waiting for you."

They spoke for hours after that, about everything and nothing. Deepankur and Senthil came up in conversation, and KK laughed as he described his two best friends—Deepankur, the dreamer with a heart of gold, and Senthil, the practical joker who always knew how to make him laugh when things seemed darkest.

"Deepankur always says," KK continued with a chuckle, "that I'm destined for greatness. But Senthil..." He paused. "Senthil believes in me when no one else does."

Swati listened with rapt attention, sharing stories of her own life, her family, and her friends. The night slipped away unnoticed as they spoke until the first rays of the morning sun began to creep in through KK's window.

"I should get some sleep," Swati said reluctantly. "You have work tomorrow, right?"

"Yeah," KK sighed, his heart heavy. "But I don't want this call to end."

"Then don't," she replied softly. "We'll talk again."

And so, they reluctantly said their goodbyes, but neither of them was willing to hang up first. There was something in the air between them—an unspoken promise that they had both found something worth holding onto.

Life was heavy, a weight I couldn't bear,
Then you walked in, and it was like breathing fresh air.
Your presence eased the chaos in my mind,
With you, I found peace I thought I'd never find.

* * * * *

Chapter 10

When Love Paints the Sky

The world outside was constantly shifting—people coming and going, cities bustling with life, and the mundane noises of everyday living. Yet in the small, tender space between KK and Swati, time had slowed. The phone calls; the long, drawn-out texts; the moments of silence shared in between words—everything had wrapped them in a cocoon of anticipation, yearning, and love.

Their relationship had blossomed from late-night phone calls and messages to real, tangible moments. What started as words on a screen—questions, fears, desires, and dreams—had now become shared smiles, intimate glances, and soft words spoken face-to-face. They had moved beyond the safety of their texts on Yoindia and Yahoo Messenger into a world where every conversation, every look, was charged with meaning. At first, it was just harmless banter, nothing more than passing time, a way to kill the loneliness of their separate worlds. But slowly, gradually, something deeper took root. They found themselves looking forward to every text, every call.

The distance between Delhi and Indore didn't seem like miles anymore. It was just a number, a fleeting obstacle. The real distance they were bridging was the one that lay between their hearts—one message at a time.

It had taken months, but one day, Swati called him; her voice trembling yet soft, like the whisper of a breeze before a thunderstorm.

"KK..." she said. He could hear the quiet sincerity in her tone, "I think I've fallen for you."

The words hung in the air like the sweetest melody, reaching deep into KK's heart. His heart, which had been cautious and reserved for so long, suddenly beat louder, faster, as if it were finally awake, finally alive.

How could something so simple, so ordinary, mean so much?

He had waited for these words like a starving man waits for food, but hearing them now, they felt like the fulfillment of something greater, something he couldn't even name.

"I've fallen for you too, Swati," he whispered, his voice breaking. God, how long had he been waiting to say that?

It wasn't just love—it was more. It was a deep, resounding certainty that the universe had brought them together for something greater than either of them could fully grasp.

But just as love began to bloom, the distance between them loomed large once again. Swati was still in Indore, finishing her physiotherapy degree, and KK, bound by his job in Delhi, was aching with the thought of not being able to hold her. Every day without her felt like an eternity. They talked endlessly about their future—how they would bridge the gap, how they would make it work. But with each passing day, the reality of their situation became clearer: how could they be together when they were separated by an entire city?

And so, their love lived between texts,
In the spaces where silence crept.
Where hearts spoke louder than words could say,
And time slipped by in its own way.

It was in those conversations that KK's mind raced for solutions. They weren't just talking anymore; they were making plans, mapping out a life, no matter the cost. He asked Swati for her CV and took it upon himself to tweak and perfect it, sending it to every hospital he knew in Delhi, making sure it found its way to the right people. Every hospital, every email, every phone call KK made was driven by a single purpose—to bring Swati to him.

Swati, ever the fighter, was determined. She wasn't going to just leave Indore. No, she needed a job to build herself in Delhi, a place of her own. She told KK about her plans and her dreams, and together they saw it—her future was no longer confined to the boundaries of Indore.

In the distance, her heart called out,
While he reached back, without a doubt.
They spoke of futures, a shared dream,
A life where nothing could tear them apart, it seemed.

As Swati neared the end of her graduation, KK knew something big was about to happen. What he didn't know was how big. Swati, always the quiet storm, had kept a secret. While she'd told KK about her plans to attend a wedding in Dehradun, she was secretly planning something entirely different—her move to Delhi, for good.

Four days had passed with no word from her, and KK was consumed with anxiety. Was she pulling away? Was this the end? He couldn't bear the thought of losing her, but he also knew he had to wait, and not make the same mistakes he had before. He spent those days in turmoil, fighting with himself, battling his instincts to call her, to demand answers. But he held on.

Days passed in silence, a storm within,
His heart heavy with the weight of what could have been.
He waited, not daring to break the spell,
Afraid that this silence might end it all as well.

On the fifth day, he awoke to a message from Swati, and his heart leaped into his throat.

"Are you in the office?"

His fingers trembled as he typed back, "No, but why?"

Her reply was simple but filled with intent: "I wanted to talk about us. But don't worry; go to work and we'll talk in the evening."

At that moment, KK felt a flood of relief. She was still there. She was still his. His mind once lost in a sea of fear, now found its way back to solid ground.

Later that day, as KK sat in a meeting, his mind wandered back to that message. She wants to talk about us. She's still thinking about us. He couldn't wait to see her, to hear her voice, to be with her.

At around 12:30 pm, during a meeting, a peon came into the room.

"There's someone to see you," he said.

"I'll be right out," KK replied, assuming it was a candidate for an interview. He finished the meeting, his thoughts lingering on Swati, wondering. But when he stepped into the reception, the sight that greeted him made his heart stop.

There she was, sitting in the chair, reading a novel. The sight of her—so calm, so beautiful, so real—made everything else fade away.

"How... how are you here?" KK stammered, unable to process what was happening.

She smiled, her eyes sparkling, and stood up. "I thought you might be missing me. So I came to surprise you."

Her words were simple, but they struck him like a thunderclap. This wasn't just love—this was a promise, a commitment. She had come to him. She had made the leap. For him.

And for the first time in their relationship, Swati stepped into his world—his office, his life, the place where he had been trying to keep a piece of himself apart from her.

KK showed her around his office and introduced her to his besties, Deepankur and Senthil. He made sure she was comfortable and reassured her that this was her world too. But it was when he asked for a half-day leave to be with her, his heart swelled with joy.

Swati had come to Delhi. She had a job. She had made the sacrifice to be with him.

And the world stood still, just for them,
Two souls entwined in a silent hymn.
In that moment, they knew no fear,
For love had brought them closer here.

And just when KK thought his heart couldn't hold any more joy, Swati dropped another bombshell.

She had found a PG in South Delhi. She was here, living in this city, starting her life.

KK could barely contain his happiness. His mind raced, and the words he could never say all came tumbling out in a rush. "Can I… Can I invite my friends to celebrate tonight? To have dinner?"

Swati, ever practical, hesitated. "It's not a big deal, KK…"

But he wouldn't take no for an answer. "Please, let me do this. It's a small thing, but it's important to me."

That night, as they dined, Deepankur and Senthil teased him mercilessly. KK sat back, watching Swati laugh. His heart ached in the most beautiful way. She was here, with him. And that was all that mattered.

Later, as the night ended and KK dropped Swati off at her PG, he couldn't resist buying her a few things for her room. "I just… I want to take care of you," he said as if it were the most natural thing in the world.

And she smiled, not resisting, not pushing him away, but accepting this gift of care and love, with the grace that had captured his heart from the very beginning.

Their communication didn't stop. It was relentless now, constant. They spoke every day, about everything. They joked about their future, about their kids, about the little things—about how many times they would make the other laugh. They would talk for hours, about everything and nothing at all.

And the days stretched into nights,
Filled with love's endless flights.
The future, once a distant dream,
Now danced within their shared scheme.

But amidst all this joy, there was one thing that KK could never seem to understand—his own reflection.

Before Swati entered his life, he was a simple man—barely aware of the mirror, never caring much about the way he looked or dressed. Clothes were just clothes, nothing more. But Swati, with her grace and elegance, had changed everything.

She wasn't just the love of his life; she was the spark that ignited the best parts of him. KK had never cared for fashion or style before; he had been the guy who wore whatever was most comfortable, never once thinking about how he looked. But Swati changed that. She would drag him to stores, picking out clothes that suited his frame, pulling him out of his comfort zone and into something new.

She made him see himself differently—

Not just the man he was,

But the man he could be.

The world around them continued to move, but for KK and Swati, time had come to a halt.

They were on the edge of something bigger—something that no distance could break, no trial could diminish. KK no longer cared about the future because it was already here, in the present, wrapped in the arms of the girl who had come into his life and turned it upside down. The man who had been hesitant to love, to give, to risk had found his everything. And that, he knew, was the greatest gift of all.

Swati had made him believe again, in love, in life, in second chances. They had fought for each other, against every odd, against every distance.

* * * * *

Chapter 11

Love Ruins

It was the kind of love that felt like destiny. A love that bloomed quietly between them, in the simplest of ways, like a secret shared in whispers. It was a love that stretched across Delhi's chaotic streets like a wide canvas, painted with stolen moments—laughter shared in empty cafes, the soft rhythm of their footsteps on evening walks, random coffee dates that stretched into hours, and movies watched in the early hours of the morning. KK and Swati's love had grown so deep that it became a song only they knew how to sing, a melody that reverberated in the deepest corners of their hearts. It was the kind of love that everyone dreams of, but few ever find.

Their relationship had been seamless and peaceful—a rare and beautiful harmony that unfolded with an ease neither of them had ever imagined. There were no fights and no misunderstandings, just a quiet understanding, a certainty that they were meant to be together. Swati wasn't just his love; she had become his heartbeat, the air he breathed, and the very soul of his existence. After years of searching and surviving through heartbreak and betrayals, he had found the love he had always longed for, a love that felt pure and untainted. It was everything he had dreamed of, everything he had never dared to hope for.

Swati's birthday arrived, and KK was determined to make it unforgettable. For weeks, he poured himself into planning the perfect surprise for her. He had chosen the beautiful Haveli Restaurant in Sector 16, Noida—a place that shimmered with history and warmth, just like the love they had. Fairy lights twinkled softly around the room, her favorite flowers filled every corner, and a cake carefully chosen to match her tastes stood at the center of it all. Even the invitation he had crafted had a personal touch—a quirky online invitation that made them both laugh and made their friends smile.

When Swati walked in, her breath caught in her throat. She was overwhelmed by the sheer beauty of it all. She hadn't experienced anything like this before, not even in her wildest dreams. At that moment, she realized the depth of KK's love—not just in the grand gestures, but in the quiet, thoughtful details that he had painstakingly put together. He had made her feel like she was the center of the universe, someone worth fighting for.

Tears filled her eyes as she rushed into his arms. "This... this is the best birthday I've ever had," she whispered, her voice choked with emotion. Time seemed to freeze in that perfect moment. KK's heart swelled with pride, knowing that he had given her something that would remain with her forever— a memory, a feeling, something that no one could ever take away.

The party ended with laughter, joy, and music that filled the air long after the guests had left. But Swati's happiness lingered, like a warm glow in her heart. In her soul, she knew that this was more than just a relationship—it was a bond, a promise that had grown deeper than anything she had ever known.

KK had yet to tell his family, knowing that his revelation would forever change everything. And so, the moment came—his sister's wedding. The perfect opportunity to introduce Swati to his family, to show them the girl who had become the center of his world.

He invited her to the wedding, eager for her to witness the beginning of the future they would share together. But there was a catch—Swati lived in a PG, and to attend an overnight marriage function, she needed her parents' approval. After much persuasion, her mother finally gave the green signal, and Swati stepped into KK's life in ways she hadn't imagined. While Swati's father had no clue about it.

On the day of the wedding, Swati wasn't just a guest—she was family. She moved through the day with such grace, helping KK's sister with the rituals, gathering gifts, and laughing with his relatives, all while wearing a smile that lit up the room. In that moment, KK realized something profound—Swati wasn't just a part of his future; she was already part of his present. She had woven herself into the fabric of his life, and his heart swelled with the quiet realization that he had found someone who would be by his side forever.

That evening, after the celebrations had settled down, KK finally found the courage to speak the words he had kept locked inside for so long. He sat down with his parents and told them, "I'm in love with Swati. I want to marry her."

The room was silent. His parents looked at him with wide eyes, their disbelief palpable. But they didn't say no. Instead, they told him, "We'll talk about it."

That night, the entire family knew. Word spread like wildfire through the wedding, and soon everyone knew that KK had chosen Swati to be his life partner. And everyone treated her as if she already belonged to them—welcoming her with open arms, making her feel loved and valued. KK could hardly believe it. He had dreamed of this moment for so long, and now, it was finally real. Swati wasn't just a dream—she was his reality. She was everything he had ever wanted, and now, she was his to love forever. Swati enjoyed the attention she got and loved the warmth of love she was getting from KK's family and relatives.

A few days later, Swati had to return to Dehradun to visit her family as she decided to share about their relationship with her family. The distance between them, even for a short time, felt unbearable. But they stayed connected through late-night calls, texts, and moments of comfort. Every conversation made them feel closer as if their love had become an invisible thread pulling them closer together.

And yet, even the most perfect of loves is tested by the harshness of reality. Fate, as it always does, had other plans. But as quickly as the joy had come, the storm began to roll in.

Her father, a stern, traditional man, had always envisioned a different future for her—one that adhered to family tradition and honor. When Swati told him about KK, he was silent for a long time, a look of disapproval spreading across his face. "Why him, Swati? You're my daughter, and I want the best for you. He is not the right choice."

Her mother, on the other hand, was more understanding but helpless. She could see the love in Swati's eyes but could not stand up to her husband's demands. However, the reality of their lives—families, traditions, expectations—was relentless. Swati's father's cold, authoritarian presence became a constant barrier between them, his pride and rigid views creating an invisible wall they could never quite break through. Every conversation with her father was a reminder of the deep rift between them. KK, who had always seen himself as an open, loving man, felt his very identity challenged. He was everything Swati needed in her eyes, yet in the eyes of her family, he was not enough. The emotional strain began to show on Swati—she began to withdraw, avoiding certain conversations with KK. Her smile was not as bright and touch, not as warm.

Life, as it often does, began to test them in ways they never expected. Swati's family dynamics, steeped in traditional values, began to cast shadows on their sunny love. Swati, caught between the love she had for KK and the obligations to her family, started to feel torn, like a leaf caught between two winds. It was a feeling she couldn't quite put into words—her heart wanted to be with KK, but her family's expectations loomed large, like a wall she couldn't scale.

But in those quiet moments of fear, Swati would sometimes turn to him and whisper, "I don't want to lose you. You are my home." And for a fleeting second, the storm would quieten in both their hearts, and they would believe, if only for a moment, that their love could defy everything.

KK noticed the change. Her voice on the phone was quieter, her texts shorter. They had always been so open with each other, but now there were pauses in their conversations as if both were waiting for something to change. The weight of her family's disapproval bore down on her shoulders, and KK could feel her slipping away, like sand running through his fingers. He watched helplessly, unable to reach her the way he used to.

The arguments began between KK and Swati after strong opposition from Swati's father. It wasn't because they no longer loved each other but because love had suddenly become a battlefield. Swati's father had made it clear that he would never accept their union, and KK, torn between his love for her and his helplessness to change her father's mind, began to break.

But despite everything, Swati never stopped loving him. In every fight, in every tear-filled argument, she would hold him close, whispering, "I'm with you. I'm always with you." Her embrace became his refuge, a place where the storm inside him could calm, where he could forget everything but her. She was his peace, the quiet anchor that kept him from losing himself in the chaos.

But as much as they fought, destiny was a powerful force that they couldn't overcome.

Swati's parents, relentless in their pressure, finally succeeded in breaking her. They made her promise to end things with KK. At first, she fought it, but the weight of their demands broke her. She called KK, asking for "just a little more time."

"I can wait forever for you," he said, his voice cracking with the weight of his love. "But I can't live without you."

Despite their promises, things deteriorated. Swati's father, stubborn and authoritative, refused to relent, and Swati was forced to return to Dehradun. The distance between them became an insurmountable gap, and their hearts broke a little more every day.

The day Swati finally broke the news, it felt like the world had crumbled beneath their feet. Her eyes were filled with sorrow, torn between love and duty. "I can't go against my family, KK," she whispered. "I'm sorry. I have to let you go."

But even from miles away, KK refused to let go. He called her, messaged her, and begged her to talk to him, to fight for them. After a month, Swati, determined to find a way to see him, convinced her family to allow her to relocate back to Delhi for her career. At least, she thought, they could see each other, even if they couldn't speak openly.

KK, desperate to have her back, would stand outside her PG day after day, just hoping for a glimpse of her. He put his job at risk, waiting for just a single moment to see her face. But every time, he only saw her eyes, wet with unshed tears—tears that he could never touch, never comfort.

His friends, Senthil and Deepankur, saw the toll it was taking on KK. They did everything in their power to bridge the gap, to bring them back together. But nothing could stop the inevitable.

In a desperate attempt to end his suffering, Senthil and Deepankur did something drastic. They called Swati and told her that KK had committed suicide.

The news shattered her, broke her into a thousand pieces. She begged her father to let her go to him one last time, desperate to see him, to say goodbye. When she arrived, breathless with grief, she found out it was all a lie. KK was alive, but the damage had already been done.

Swati's father, furious beyond reason, demanded that she leave Delhi immediately. And this time, Swati complied.

They never spoke again.

Days turned into weeks. Weeks turned into months. KK fell into a deep depression, a black hole that consumed him from the inside. He withdrew from everything—from the world, from love, from life itself. He roamed the streets aimlessly, his heart a hollow shell. He had lost her.

Then, years later, just as he had almost convinced himself never to love again, an e-card arrived from Swati. The message was simple, but it tore through him like a knife:

"I'm sorry for everything. I still love you. But my marriage has been arranged."

And with those words, the last piece of KK's heart shattered.

And so, in silence, I stand,
The love I held slipping through my hands.
A promise made, a love once true,
Now a memory, fading like morning dew"

KK knew, at that moment, that he would never love again—not the way he had loved Swati. She had been his everything, and now she was gone.

And so, he closed the door on his heart forever, holding onto the memory of a love that was never meant to be.

The pain in KK's heart was unbearable. His heart thudded loudly in his ears, and for a moment, he thought he might collapse. How could she say goodbye after all they had shared? How could she walk away from him, from their love? But the answer was clear: love wasn't always enough. There were too many forces beyond their control, and the harsh reality of those forces came crashing down like a tidal wave.

Swati, with tears running down her face, walked away from him that day, her back slowly fading into the distance. But the memory of her lingered in the air around him, in every corner of his world. He tried to move on, to tell himself that she was just another chapter in his life. But the truth was, every love after her felt incomplete. His heart was broken, but it was still hers. He couldn't let go.

The nights felt heavier after she left, the silence almost suffocating. KK found himself reaching for a cigarette, a habit he had sworn he'd never embrace. Each drag burned his lungs, but it dulled the ache in his chest—a small distraction from the emptiness Swati's absence had carved into him. The smoke curled around him in the form of a fragile veil for his shattered heart. He wished he could exhale his pain along with the smoke. It wasn't about rebellion or escape; it was about finding a way to breathe in a world that suddenly felt too harsh without her.

His mother watched from the doorway, her heart breaking with every puff of smoke that rose into the air.

She saw the boy she had raised with so much love slipping into a void she couldn't reach. Tears welled up in her eyes as she silently prayed for his healing, wishing she could shoulder even a fragment of his pain. But there was very little she could do. Words felt hollow, and comfort seemed elusive. All she could do was stand by him, hoping that the storm within him would pass and that the love she had given him all these years would guide him back to himself.

On the balcony, with a cigarette's glow,
I grieve for a love I'll never know,
Smoke rise high, where dreams once soared,
Ashes fall, where my heart is stored.

He learned to live, but he never truly lived again. In moments of quiet reflection, he would think of her, wonder about the life she had built, the man she had married, and wonder if, deep down, she ever thought of him. But he never reached out, never asked. Because, in a way, he knew—sometimes love isn't meant to be. Sometimes love is just a lesson, a moment in time that leaves behind the bittersweet taste of a life not lived.

"I thought love was eternal, but her goodbye taught me it is transient like holding sand—no matter how tightly I held, she slipped through my hands."

* * * * *

Chapter 12

The Heart That Refused to Learn

KK's life had become a routine, one that no longer offered excitement or hope. After a decade of heartbreaks, he had learned to shut down his emotions, to lock away the parts of him that still believed in love. Back-to-back failures in love had made him cynical, and over time, he convinced himself that the pursuit of money and a career would fill the void that love had left behind.

Love, they say, is worth the pain,
But every wound it leaves, I can't explain.
Is it better to love or to stay alone?
When the heart, once broken, turns to stone?

He no longer interacted with girls unless absolutely necessary for work. His relationships had taught him one hard lesson: love only brought pain. And so, his focus shifted entirely to his career. He worked relentlessly, shaping his future and climbing the corporate ladder, all the while convincing himself that success, wealth, and power were the only things that mattered. He believed that money could buy everything—respect, influence, and even love.

He became a well-known figure in his organization, recognized for his exceptional work; he had become the go-to person for anyone seeking guidance. His colleagues, from junior interns to senior leaders, found in him a mentor, a problem-solver, and a friend. His boss, a renowned CIO, took him under her wing, guiding him like a son, always keen on nurturing his potential. His entire world revolved around his work, and nothing else seemed to matter.

But fate, as it often does, had other plans for him.

After nearly two years, a girl named Samriddhi entered his life like a breath of fresh air, though KK hardly noticed at first. She was an intern in the HR department, and their interactions were brief and mainly related to work. Samriddhi was nothing like the girl who had previously caught his attention—she had no extravagant style or air of sophistication. Instead, she was simple, with excessively oily hair, glasses that seemed too big for her face, and a complexion that spoke of a middle-class upbringing. KK saw her as just another face in the crowd, someone who wasn't even close to the type of girl he'd once been drawn to.

In the crowd, you seemed so plain,
A simple soul amidst the strain.
Yet little did I know, inside,
A heart would blossom, far and wide.

But work brought them together, and soon Samriddhi was seeking his guidance more and more. They'd have lunch together, exchange pleasantries, brainstorm ideas for office events, and discuss work strategies. Though she was always grateful for his support, KK didn't think much of their connection. She was just another colleague.

One day, however, something changed. As he rushed to the office canteen to grab his breakfast, he noticed Samriddhi sitting alone, her face hidden behind her phone. There was something different in the way she was holding it, her shoulders shaking ever so slightly. When she hung up, he could see the tears in her eyes. She didn't notice him at first, but KK couldn't shake the image of her fragile form, something inside him tugging at his heart.

He thought about ignoring it, but a voice inside told him to reach out.

That evening, he called her. "Samriddhi, what happened today? Why did you leave so suddenly?" he asked, trying to sound casual.

"I just had some things to take care of," she replied, her voice trembling ever so slightly.

"Are you okay?" KK asked, his concern for her growing despite himself.

But Samriddhi was quick to shut him out. She didn't want to talk about it, and she didn't owe him an explanation. He respected her space and decided not to press further.

The next day, during another work session, he asked again, more gently this time, "Are you sure you're okay? You seemed really upset yesterday."

Samriddhi shifted uncomfortably, then changed the subject, avoiding his question completely. KK, sensing her discomfort, promised himself he wouldn't bring it up again. And he didn't.

Days passed and the distance between them grew. Samriddhi had clearly noticed the shift in KK's behavior—he was no longer the friendly, supportive mentor he once was. She didn't know why he had distanced himself, but she couldn't help but feel the pang of regret. She had pushed him away, and now their friendship felt strained.

Then one evening, Samriddhi called him unexpectedly.

"I need your help, KK," she said, her voice wavering. "But... can we talk first?"

"What's wrong?" he asked, his tone softer now, sensing the urgency in her words.

"I'm sorry for not answering you earlier," Samriddhi said. "I just... I don't like sharing personal stuff. But trust me when I say I didn't want to hurt you."

KK was silent for a moment. "Samriddhi, just tell me what help you need?"

"I... I'm in a relationship," she began, her voice thick with emotion. "I'm in love with someone, but... he doesn't love me back. At least, not in the way I want him to. He insults me, makes fun of me in front of his friends, and refuses to acknowledge my feelings. And when I tried to talk to him about it, he just ignored me. Yesterday, we had a huge fight, and he hasn't called me since."

The words hit KK like a storm. He didn't know how to respond. Part of him wanted to comfort her, tell her she deserved better. But another part of him—one he wasn't ready to admit—felt the sting of his own unspoken emotions.

"I'm sorry, Samriddhi," he finally said, his voice low. "I don't know what to tell you. But if he's treating you this way, maybe it's time you asked yourself whether you deserve someone like that."

Samriddhi didn't respond, but the silence between them spoke volumes. He knew she wasn't ready to let go. Love, it seemed, had a hold on her that was stronger than reason.

As Samriddhi spoke more about her situation, KK began to understand that the issue was not just her relationship. It was the pressure from her family. Samriddhi's parents, especially her mother, had long pushed her toward marriage. They wanted her to find a stable and secure life with a man who could provide for her, and this relationship, despite the abuse, had been what they expected. They didn't know the truth—her boyfriend's cruel behavior, the emotional neglect, and the strain on her self-esteem. Her mother had often told her to endure for the sake of the family, to hold on because 'every marriage has struggles'. But Samriddhi felt torn. She was caught between her duty to her family, their expectations for her to marry this man, and her own painful reality.

Torn between love and duty's chain,
A heart burdened with unseen pain.
Family's voice calls out in the night,
But the heart knows only one truth—what's right.

Weeks later, during a team outing to Gurgaon, Samriddhi approached him again. She wanted to talk, and despite his initial resistance, KK listened. In the serene backdrop of the resort, she poured her heart out. Her voice trembled as she spoke of the years she had spent trying to earn her boyfriend's love, only to be met with disdain. Her vulnerability struck a chord in KK. He saw glimpses of his own past in her pain, a mirror to the wounds he had tried so hard to forget.

Their conversations grew deeper after that day. Late-night calls turned into confessions of fears and dreams. KK, despite himself, began to care for her. Was KK falling in love with her? He had no answer to it. He wanted to take it slowly as within his heart he was not sure of the answer. When their office team planned a trip to Shirdi, Samriddhi hesitated but eventually decided to join, seeking solace in the companionship of her colleagues—especially KK.

On the train, fate placed them in the same compartment. Under the dim light of the cabin, KK found himself unable to resist. He reached for her hand and confessed, “I don’t know how or when, but I’ve fallen for you,” he said, his voice steady yet vulnerable. “I know you’re in love with someone else, and I know I have no place in your heart. But I couldn’t keep this to myself anymore.”

Samriddhi looked at him, wide-eyed. For a moment, there was silence, and then she whispered, “KK, I’m already in love with someone else. I can’t leave him.”

The words hit KK like a dagger, though he had braced himself for rejection. He managed a weak smile. “I’ll make you fall in love with me. Maybe not today, but someday,” he said, half-joking, half-pleading. But the atmosphere had grown cold, the warmth of their camaraderie replaced by an awkward silence.

I will wait for you, no matter how long,
I’ll sing you a love that’s pure and strong.
In your heart’s silence, I’ll be the sound,
In your lost world, I’ll be the ground.

That night, as she slept, KK couldn’t take his eyes off her. She looked peaceful, her face free of the burdens she carried during the day. Noticing that she was shivering, he quietly draped his blanket over her. In the morning, when she saw the second blanket, her eyes softened, but her words remained cautious. “You’re the best friend I could ever have," she said, her voice warm but distant.

The trip continued, filled with laughter and shared moments, but KK's heart grew heavier with each passing day. On the final day of the trip, as they prepared to leave, Samriddhi looked at KK with an intensity that made his breath catch. "KK," she said softly, "you've set a benchmark for what care and respect should feel like. I don't know what to do with these feelings."

When they returned to Delhi, he dropped her home. Her parting words echoed in his mind: "I need time to think... but you've left a mark on me."

"Take all the time you need," KK replied, forcing a smile. "I'll always be here for you."

KK watched her leave, his heart heavy yet hopeful. That night, he wrote in his journal:

"Her laughter is my melody, her sadness my ache. She doesn't see it yet, but her happiness is my purpose. Even if I'm just a shadow in her story, I'll be the one that never fades."

As the cab drove away, KK felt a hollow ache in his heart. He had opened his heart again, only to be reminded of the futility of hope. He replayed her words, searching for meaning, for a thread of possibility, even as he knew deep down that her answer would never change.

In the quiet of his room that night, he wrote:

A heart once mended is a fragile thing,
It breaks anew with the faintest sting.
I dared to hope, to dream, to feel,
Only to learn that love won't heal.

KK laughed bitterly at himself. He had been a fool to believe in something he had sworn off long ago. Love, it seemed, was a lesson he was destined to relearn the hard way, again and again. Samriddhi continued to lean on KK, unaware of the quiet storms he weathered for her. And KK, true to his nature, gave everything he had, knowing that some battles are lost before they begin.

* * * * *

Chapter 13

The Silent Refrain

Weeks passed, and KK threw himself into work, his focus sharp, his mind occupied, and yet, the ache in his heart never quite faded. The fire that once burned within him seemed to smolder now, reduced to a faint glow, its heat barely enough to warm the edges of his soul. He buried himself in spreadsheets, meetings, and deadlines, trying to outrun the gnawing emptiness that had taken root deep within him. But no matter how fast he ran, he couldn't escape it. His colleagues noticed the change—he was quieter, more withdrawn, and no longer the passionate, fiery KK they once knew.

I buried my heart in work's embrace,
But the shadows of love left no trace.
My smile, once bright, now fades with time,
As I search for peace in a silent rhyme.

Samriddhi's presence lingered in his thoughts, like a melody that wouldn't let go. Every laugh they had shared, every touch, every fleeting glance, the warmth between them, and the unspoken connection they had almost bloomed. He couldn't forget her, though she tried to maintain distance. The pull of her, the way she looked at him with those uncertain eyes, haunted him day and night.

Despite the confusion, despite the pain, KK wasn't ready to let go of her. The problem was, he wasn't sure if she felt the same.

I'm torn between hope and sorrow,
A heart that can't wait for tomorrow.
But am I just a dream in your eyes?
Or a fleeting shadow beneath your skies?

One morning, Samriddhi invited him for coffee in the office canteen. Her voice, soft and hesitant, broke through the fog that had clouded KK's heart.

"I don't think I've thanked you enough for being there for me," she began, her eyes averted, as though afraid to meet his gaze. "You're always so calm, so steady, and I feel safe around you."

KK smiled, but the weight behind his expression was heavy, a burden he carried in silence. "I'm glad you feel that way," he said quietly. "But what about you? What about your own happiness, Samriddhi? Are you truly happy with him?" The question came out more forcefully than he intended, and the instant it left his mouth, he regretted it.

Samriddhi's eyes darted to the floor, and she took a deep breath. She seemed to be wrestling with something inside her before speaking, her voice trembling. "I want to be happy, KK. But I don't know how to be without him. I've been with him for so long, and I'm scared that if I let go, I'll have nothing left."

His heart shattered at her words. He wanted to pull her close to tell her everything would be okay. But instead, he masked his pain with a soft chuckle as though the words were nothing. "You don't need to hold onto something just because it's familiar. You're worth more than someone who makes you feel this way. You deserve someone who sees you and understands the depth of your soul. You deserve more than the shadows of the past."

She looked at him, her eyes filled with gratitude and confusion. "But I can't—"

Before she could finish, KK gently placed his finger on her lips, silencing her. "I know. It's not easy to move on from something you've invested so much in. But that doesn't mean you can't start a new chapter, one where you choose your own happiness."

The silence that followed felt heavy with the weight of unsaid words, but something shifted in that moment. She reached out, her hand gently clasping his. The connection between them was undeniable, more real than anything he had ever known.

In your hand, I find my way,
A path I never thought would stay.
The road ahead, unclear and wide,
But in your eyes, I choose to confide.

The next few days passed with a quiet, uncertain tension. Samriddhi seemed more distant, her internal struggles weighing on her like an anchor. KK respected her need for space, but something inside him told him that she was pulling away—not because she didn't care, but because she was afraid to confront the truths hidden deep within her heart.

Then, one morning, she sent him a message that shattered the fragile calm between them.

"I've decided to end things with him. I don't know what the future holds, but I can't keep living in the past. Thank you for giving me the courage to do this. I'll be fine. You've done enough."

KK felt the earth tremble beneath him, his heart a mixture of relief and fear. Samriddhi had made a choice, a painful one, but it was hers to make. He could feel the weight of her decision, the strength it took to end something so familiar, so intertwined with her life. And yet, as the days passed, he couldn't shake the feeling that something was amiss. She seemed more distant than ever. Her presence was like a ghost, haunting his thoughts in the quietest moments.

They still exchanged pleasantries in the office, sat through meetings, and laughed at the occasional joke, but a gap had formed between them—one neither of them dared to cross.

And in the silence of unspoken dreams,
I find myself lost, or so it seems.
You stand there, close but far away,
A shadow lingering, night and day.

KK knew something was wrong, but he couldn't find the courage to ask. Not yet. Maybe he was afraid of the answer. Maybe he didn't want to face the truth that she was slipping through his fingers.

One evening, after an exhausting day at work, KK found himself waiting outside her office. The weight of the silence between them had grown unbearable. His heart pounded in his chest as he watched her walk past him, her face downcast and lost in thought.

"Samriddhi," he called softly, his voice carrying the weight of his concern.

She stopped but didn't meet his gaze, her body language tense. "What's wrong?" KK asked, his voice filled with the emotion he could no longer hide.

For what felt like an eternity, she didn't speak. Her lips trembled as if she were searching for the right words. Finally, she spoke, her voice barely above a whisper. "I need time, KK. More time to figure things out. I don't know what I want yet. And... and I think it's better if we stay away from each other for now."

The words hit KK like a blow to the heart. His thoughts spun wildly, a thousand emotions crashing into each other. He wanted to argue, to plead, and to tell her that he couldn't bear this distance, but he knew he had to respect her wishes.

"Okay," he said quietly, his voice shaking with a pain he couldn't mask. "But Samriddhi, don't push me away when you need someone the most. I'll always be here for you, whether or not you want me to be."

She looked at him, her eyes filled with regret, a tear threatening to fall. "I know. And I appreciate you more than you'll ever know. But this... I need to do this alone."

And with those words, she turned and walked away, leaving KK standing alone in the dimming light. His heart, once filled with hope, now felt as though it had been ripped apart. The future that once seemed so full of promise had become a vast, empty void.

You walked away, but I still remain,
Holding on to love's sweet refrain.
In the silence, I wait for you,
Not knowing what I'm meant to do.

He stood there, feeling more lost than ever, as the shadows of the past and future stretched out before him, merging into one uncertain road ahead.

* * * * *

Chapter 14

The Dance of Fate

For months, KK had been drifting. The ache in his heart never quite faded. Each passing moment felt like a tug-of-war between hope and despair, each side pulling him in opposite directions. His heart told him that Samriddhi was worth every ounce of effort, every tear, and every ounce of patience he had left to give. But his mind, well, his mind feared the inevitable. What if she never truly chose him? What if he was just a fleeting moment in her life, a temporary solace in a storm?

Despite the quiet distance that had crept between them after her decision to end things with him, something in KK refused to let go. He could sense that the walls she had built were not meant to keep him out but to protect herself from the confusion, the guilt, the weight of her past. He had always believed that love, in its purest form, was a choice—one that could not be forced, but one that could heal even the most broken heart. And if there was one thing KK had learned over the years, it was that the heart, though fragile, could be resilient when it was given the right space to heal.

The days dragged on, with Samriddhi still distant, caught in the whirlwind of her thoughts and emotions. But KK never wavered. He remained patient, always there for her, not as a savior but as someone who truly cared for her. He didn't rush her, didn't push her for answers. He simply gave her the time and space she needed to find herself. Deep down, he believed that when the time came, she would choose him.

And then, one evening, after a particularly long day, it happened.

KK was sitting in his office, staring at his computer screen without really seeing it. His thoughts were miles away, with her, as they often were. He had come to a place where he accepted the uncertainty of the situation. He had no idea what the future held, but he knew one thing for certain—he couldn't imagine a life without her.

His phone buzzed, pulling him from his thoughts. The message was from Samriddhi.

"Can we talk?"

His heart skipped a beat. Yes. This was it. He didn't waste a moment in replying.

"Of course. When and where?"

Within minutes, she had sent him the address of a small café they had once visited together during a conference. He had almost forgotten about that day—how everything had felt so easy, so natural between them.

He had hoped that one day they would return there, but he never expected it to happen like this.

He arrived early and tried to calm the nervous excitement building within him. He took a seat by the window, his fingers tapping restlessly on the table. The café was quiet; the soft murmur of conversations and clinking cups created a peaceful ambiance.

And then she walked in.

Samriddhi looked just as beautiful as ever, but there was something different about her. Her eyes, once clouded with doubt, now sparkled with something more. Something more hopeful, perhaps. As she approached him, KK stood up, and for a moment, they simply stood there, gazing at each other. The world outside seemed to vanish at that moment—there was no café, no chaos, no past or future, just the two of them.

"I've been thinking," she began, her voice soft, yet steady, "about everything. About what you said, about what we've been through... and what we could be. And I realized something. I've been holding on to the past because I was afraid. Afraid of letting go, afraid of the unknown. But I've spent so much time running away from what I truly want, that I almost missed it right in front of me."

KK's heart raced as he listened. Was this really happening?

"I was scared, KK. Scared to trust again, scared to open my heart," she continued, her eyes meeting his, vulnerability in every word. "But then I remembered everything you've shown me—the patience, the understanding, and the love you've given without expecting anything in return. You've always believed in me, even when I couldn't believe in myself."

A tear slid down her cheek, but this time, it wasn't one of sadness. It was a tear of release, of finally allowing herself to feel the love she had pushed away for so long. KK reached out instinctively, wiping it away gently with his thumb.

"Samriddhi, you don't have to say anything. I'm here, always. But if you choose me—if you want this—just know that I'll never ask you to change. I'll never push you to be anything you're not. I'll stand beside you, not because I want something from you, but because I want to see you happy, in every way possible. However, the only promise I need from you is not to let me go ever, no matter what the situation may be. I want to marry you," KK said as he also opened up about his previous affairs.

Her breath caught in her throat, and for a moment, she seemed to hesitate. Then, as if the weight of her decision had finally lifted, she smiled the first true smile he had seen in weeks. It was radiant, full of life and possibility.

"I want you, KK," she whispered, her voice barely audible over the hum of the café. "I want to take a chance, to let go of the past and move forward. I want to be with you, not because I need to escape, but because I finally see that I deserve happiness. And you... you're the one who makes me feel like I can have it."

KK felt like his world had just shifted. The uncertainty that had clouded his heart lifted, and he could finally breathe again. He took her hand in his; his heart was full of gratitude and joy. "You don't have to be afraid anymore, Samriddhi. We're in this together."

And in that moment, with the weight of the world finally lifted from their shoulders, they knew that this was the beginning of something new—a love born not from desperation, but from choice, patience, and trust. They had both been through the fire, but now, they could rise from it, together.

As they walked out of the café, hand in hand, KK couldn't help but think of all the trials they had faced, the struggles, the uncertainty, and how, in the end, love had found its way to them.

In the darkness, we found the light,
In the silence, we made it right.
Love wasn't meant to be easy, I see,
But with you, I'll be all I'm meant to be.

And after a long time, KK felt whole once again. Not because of what he had gained but because of what they had built together. Their future was uncertain, yes, but now it was something they would face together, side by side. And that in itself was enough.

* * * * *

Chapter 15

A Heart Torn Asunder

The past two years of KK and Samriddhi's love story had been a whirlwind of emotions—an unfiltered canvas of laughter, warmth, arguments, and dreams. From sneaking moments in the office canteen to celebrating birthdays with shared cake slices, their love blossomed against the mundane rhythm of daily life. They had been each other's solace, building a fortress of trust that seemed unbreakable. It was a relationship that had blossomed amidst shared coffee breaks, stolen glances, and endless conversations under the dim office lights. Samriddhi was everything KK had ever wished for—a girl who radiated confidence and kindness in equal measure. She was his muse, his best friend, and his anchor in a life that was often marred by disappointments. Their love had not only flourished between them but had become the talk of their office. Colleagues fondly referred to Samriddhi as 'Bhabhi', and there were days when KK would be teased mercilessly, turning him red with embarrassment. Yet, amidst the camaraderie and office banter, a silent, unspoken question began to grow—what next? Would their love story culminate in a happily-ever-after, or was it destined to remain a fleeting chapter in the book of KK's life forever?

In quiet moments, his heart wrote unspoken verses:

In the glow of her smile, I find my sun,"
Yet, in her silences, fears quietly run.
Will this love, so pure, endure the storm?
Or fade like a shadow, fleeting and forlorn?

KK had now turned 27, and the societal and familial pressure to get married loomed heavily over him. Every phone call from relatives, every casual family dinner, brought subtle hints, veiled questions, and direct nudges. "It's time, KK," his mother would say, her voice laced with both worry and hope. While KK deeply respected his family's wishes, he knew his heart belonged to Samriddhi. Yet, after years of heartbreak and betrayal, he was cautious. He needed certainty, not just from Samriddhi but also from her family, before taking the plunge.

One evening, while on a date at their favorite café, sitting in a cozy corner with soft yellow lights and the aroma of freshly brewed coffee, KK decided to bring up the topic. His heart raced as he looked into Samriddhi's eyes, a mix of apprehension and hope clouding his expression. "Samriddhi," he began, his voice steady yet vulnerable, "my family wants me to get married. They've been waiting, and I don't want to keep them in the dark anymore. But before I tell them about us, I need to know—are you ready to stand by me? Will your family accept us?"

Samriddhi listened intently, her face a canvas of emotions—surprise, anxiety, and a quiet determination.

"KK," she said softly, reaching out to hold his hand, "you can tell your family that we're together and that we want to marry. I've always believed in us, and it's time my parents know too. I'll speak to them this weekend. It's not going to be easy, but it's a conversation I can't keep avoiding."

KK's heart penned verses as he walked home:

Her words were a flame in the night,
Banishing doubts with their radiant light.
Yet beneath the warmth, a shadow grew,
Whispering fears of what he might lose.

The weekend brought a mix of excitement and anxiety. Samriddhi kept her word and spoke to her parents, who, to her surprise, were willing to meet KK's family. Their initial hesitation seemed to dissolve as Samriddhi's conviction shone through. She shared the news with KK, whose joy knew no bounds. The next day, KK informed his family about Samriddhi. While there was initial resistance, his mother, who had witnessed KK's struggles and heartbreaks, convinced the family to give this relationship a chance.

The following week was a flurry of preparations. KK and Samriddhi spent hours discussing how to ensure everything went smoothly. There was laughter, hope, and dreams of a future together. Samriddhi expressed her desire to continue supporting her sisters' education and her family even after marriage. KK, with his characteristic warmth, replied, "Is that all you want? Of course, I'll support them too." Their bond felt unshakable, a partnership built on mutual respect and understanding.

In those cherished moments, KK wrote:

Her dreams are threads I wish to weave,
Into a tapestry of love, where none must grieve.
Her burdens are mine, her joys are my own,
In her smile, I find a home unknown.

Saturday morning arrived, the day when both families were to meet. KK's home was abuzz with activity. His mother ensured everything was perfect, from the snacks to the seating arrangements. KK, dressed in his best attire, waited nervously, stealing glances at the clock. By 11:00 am, excitement turned into mild concern as there was no sign of Samriddhi's family. But as the clock ticked past noon, their excitement turned to worry; they hadn't arrived. KK's calls to Samriddhi went unanswered, and with each passing minute, his heart sank a little deeper. KK's mother saw his losing hope. She added to comfort his peace of soul, "Don't worry, they may have got some unexpected guests at home."

Finally, at 5:00 pm, KK's phone buzzed. It was Samriddhi. Her voice was trembling, heavy with suppressed sobs. "KK," she began, "I'm so sorry. We couldn't make it today." KK, though relieved to hear her voice, couldn't hide his disappointment. "It's okay, Samriddhi," he said gently. "We can reschedule." But Samriddhi's next words unsettled him. "My parents want to meet you first, without your family. I don't know why, but I have a bad feeling about this."

KK, ever the optimist, reassured her. "Don't worry, Sona. I'll meet them and win their hearts. Trust me." Despite his comforting words, a knot of unease began to form in his heart.

That night, KK wrote what felt like a lament:

If the stars above must write my fate,
Why must their ink decide my fate?
If love is bound by celestial threads,
Then why do hearts break when vows are said?

A few days later, Samriddhi arranged for KK to meet her parents at a nearby restaurant. He arrived early, his nerves on edge. When they finally walked in, KK stood respectfully, bowing slightly in greeting. Samriddhi's mother, dressed immaculately in a sari, offered a faint smile, while her father's eyes appraised KK like a banker evaluating a risky investment.

The questions began, each one cutting deeper than the last.

"Do you have a car?"

"No, sir, not yet. I rely on public transport and rickshaws."

"What's your salary?"

"5.5 lakh per annum," KK replied, his voice steady despite the rising tension.

Samriddhi's mother exchanged a glance with her husband before asking, "Do you think that's enough to take care of our daughter?"

KK swallowed hard but answered truthfully. "I'm working toward better opportunities. I want to give Samriddhi everything she deserves."

Her father leaned forward, his voice cold. "But why should we choose you for our daughter? What makes you capable of providing her the life we've given her?"

KK paused, meeting their gaze with quiet resolve. "Because I love her. I will dedicate my life to making her happy, no matter what it takes."

Days turned into weeks, and KK sensed the growing resistance from Samriddhi's family. Every step forward felt like wading through quicksand. The breaking point came when an astrologer, consulted at her mother's insistence, declared KK's horoscope as 'inauspicious'.

Samriddhi's mother seized this opportunity, using it as justification to end the match. She told KK directly, her tone sharp and dismissive, "You're not the right match for our daughter. Forget her."

The words felt like a slap, but KK refused to give up. He worked harder, securing a higher-paying job in hopes of proving himself worthy. But as he climbed the ladder of success, he found himself further distanced from the girl he loved.

Later that night, Samriddhi called, her voice trembling. "KK, they didn't approve. They think... you're not enough." The words stung, but KK held firm. "I'll win them over, Sona. Trust me." She whispered, "I trust you." That was all he needed to hold onto hope.

But days turned into battlefield. Samriddhi's parents intensified their search for a 'better' match for their daughter. Late-night calls between KK and Samriddhi became an escape from the mounting pressure. "I won't marry anyone but you," she'd say, her voice steadfast, her love unwavering.

One day, her mother agreed to meet KK again, this time at another astrologer's place. A meeting with an astrologer, orchestrated by her mother, became another nail in the coffin. The astrologer's grim predictions painted KK's life as either destined for grandeur or ruin. Her mother seized this as another reason to end their relationship.

"Is this the life you want to give my daughter?" she asked pointedly. KK's silence was deafening, his tears his only response.

Despite the rejection, KK clung to hope, living up to the promise made to Samriddhi that he would work harder, earn more, and prove himself. He landed a new job with a better salary, believing it might sway her family.

But Samriddhi's mother remained adamant, her disapproval now a wall between them.

Then came the ultimate betrayal. Samriddhi's unwavering love kept them afloat until one day, she lashed out at KK in the office canteen.

"How dare you insult my mother?" she accused, her eyes blazing.

"I... I didn't," KK stammered, shocked. "I've never spoken ill of her."

"You were always present during our calls—on speaker, remember?"

But Samriddhi, blinded by loyalty to her family, refused to believe him.

Her anger was unyielding. "Stay away from me, KK. I won't marry someone who disrespects my family."

If only she saw the tears I conceal,
The scars on a heart that struggles to heal.
But love, they say, is a gift, not a demand,
So I let her go, with an open arm.

Days turned into weeks, and silence became the new language of their love. KK's attempts to mend their bond were met with indifference. When she finally agreed to meet, it was only to deliver a heart-breaking verdict: "I want a breakup. I can't be with someone who doesn't respect my family."

Her words shattered KK, but he couldn't let go. "Please, let's visit another astrologer," he pleaded. The new astrologer painted a brighter picture, but it did little to repair the damage.

Samriddhi's mother had sown seeds of doubt, and they had taken root in Samriddhi's heart. "Don't you dare talk about my mother again," she warned, walking away for the last time.

Even as his world fell apart, KK couldn't let go of the love they had shared. He resigned from his job and was serving his notice period, hoping a fresh start might heal his shattered heart. But the final blow came when Samriddhi filed a complaint against him at work, accusing him of harassment. Though the truth of their love was known to everyone, KK chose to leave quietly, carrying the weight of a love that once promised forever but left him in pieces.

KK felt an unbearable emptiness creeping back into his life. The world around him blurred, and every sound seemed distant, muted by the weight of yet another heartbreak. He found solace in his old companion—the cigarette. Lighting it up felt like rekindling a friendship with something that understood his silence. Each drag became a momentary escape, the smoke swirling around him like a ghost of comfort. It wasn't just a habit anymore; it was his way of numbing the ache, a fleeting respite from the memories of her laughter, her touch, and the promises that now felt like lies.

Yet, even in heartbreak, KK held onto one truth: Love isn't about winning or losing. It's about giving, even when it leaves you broken. He realized that some battles, no matter how valiantly fought, are destined to be lost. His heart ached, but amidst the pain, he clung to the belief that true love was about giving, even if it meant letting go.

That night, alone in his room, KK penned a few lines:

They called it love,
But forgot its essence.
A union of souls,
Not a measure of presence.
In her laughter, I found life,
In her eyes, my every dream.
But love, it seems,
Is never what it seems.

KK folded the paper and tucked it away, a fragment of a love that was never meant to be.

"The cruelest goodbye isn't the one spoken in anger—it's the one delivered in unjust blame, where love becomes a weapon and the heart a battlefield."

* * * * *

Chapter 16

Tears in the Lap of Love

KK sat in the dim, lonely light of his independent home, the silence surrounding him like a heavy fog. It was an empty kind of silence, a silence that felt like a void, a hollow echo that only deepened the ache in his heart. The walls seemed to close in around him, the rooms stretching on forever in a quiet, suffocating prison. He exhaled deeply, the cigarette in his hand his only companion in this vast emptiness. As the smoke swirled around him, it almost seemed to mirror the chaos in his heart—rising up, fleeting, and then vanishing into nothing.

At 29, he was a man who had lost everything. Not just love, but his own identity. His face—something he had never thought much about growing up—had become a curse, a constant reminder of his unworthiness. He cursed the reflection in the mirror, the face that God had given him. To KK, it was a constant rejection, a symbol that he was undeserving of love, undeserving of affection.

The cigarette had become his closest friend in the years since the heartbreak. It was his way to fill the emptiness and dull the pain. Every drag soothed his restless mind, but never for long. It never reached the root of the sorrow. Nothing ever did.

A hollow heart, a weary soul,
A dream once bright, now dark as coal.
The face I wear, a mask of shame,
A love once sought, now lost to blame.

He had once believed that love could heal everything, that somehow, someone could look beyond his flawed exterior and see the man inside. He had been wrong. His face, the one he had learned to loathe, had turned into the very thing that kept him from ever experiencing true love. With each rejection, the wound deepened. And when Samriddhi, the one he had poured his heart into, left him without a word, the wound became a scar that would never heal.

In the beginning, he had tried to be strong. He had convinced himself that the pain would fade with time. But time was cruel. It only deepened the ache, and he found himself swallowed by it. The bitterness, the regret, the loneliness—he couldn't escape it. The cigarettes had become his way of hiding from the truth, from the world, from himself.

His family, ever so concerned, had begun to notice the change in him. They saw him retreat further into himself, the cigarette butts pile up by the window, and the empty cups of tea that sat untouched. They worried for him, for the man they had raised with so much love. They would gather around him, offering comfort and words of hope that he couldn't bring himself to believe.

"Son," his mother would say, her voice thick with concern, "you'll find someone who will love you for who you are. You will. Don't lose hope."

Her words were a balm, but the wounds ran deep,
A promise I couldn't bring myself to keep.
Love was a lie, a tale once sweet,
Now shattered and lost beneath my feet.

He had become a master at pretending, at putting on a mask, at letting the world see a version of him that was strong and together. But inside, KK was shattered. He could no longer look at himself without seeing the ugliness that others had seen for so long. He was broken, and no one could fix him—not even his family.

Days bled into weeks, and weeks into months. He shifted jobs, moving to another giant organization, hoping work would distract him. But even in the busyness of his new life, Samriddhi's memory followed him like a shadow. The quiet moments and the stillness in the air would bring it all rushing back. The love he had given so freely, the hope he had held onto so tightly—everything was gone now, slipping through his fingers like sand.

Work once again became his refuge, his escape. He buried himself in tasks, in helping others, becoming the people's champion—always smiling, hiding the pain in his heart, always offering a hand, always the one they could count on. He threw himself into work, into making others feel better, while inside, he was falling apart.

But no matter how much he worked, no matter how many cigarettes he smoked to drown out the noise, KK couldn't escape the truth—he had given up on love. He had promised himself that he would never fall for anyone again. The face God had given him wasn't meant to be loved. His life would be about helping others, not finding love for himself.

I will never love again. I've closed that door,
For love, like a thief, took all I had and more.
My face, my heart, they're not for her to see,
For love was never meant for someone like me.

His family, though silent, could sense the heaviness in his heart. They could see the light in his fading eyes. His mother, especially, watched him with such care, her heart aching for the boy she had raised. She never once asked him about marriage or pushed him to talk about love, knowing that the wounds ran too deep. But she never stopped hoping. She never stopped believing that somewhere out there, someone would see past his exterior and love him for who he was.

But as time passed, the pressure from relatives grew unbearable. His family, desperate to see their son happy again, registered him on a matrimonial site without his knowledge, hoping that somehow, something would spark.

Yet they never dared to speak of it, never dared to bring it up, fearing his rejection.

One night, KK overheard his mother talking to his father in their bedroom. She was crying, her voice shaking with worry. She didn't speak much, but her words pierced him like a knife. She was afraid for him. She wanted to talk to him about marriage, about finding someone, but she knew it would break him all over again.

KK's heart twisted in his chest. The thought that he had been the cause of tears in the eyes of the woman who had loved him unconditionally, the woman who had never once cared about his appearance, was too much for him to bear. He had hurt her. He had broken her heart. And yet, all she wanted was for him to be happy.

A mother's heart, a love so true,
It beats for the child she never knew.
Would hurt her so, would break her apart,
Yet still, she loves him with all her heart.

He couldn't sit with it anymore. His bond with his mother had always been the strongest. Now, as he saw her in pain because of him, he knew he had to do something. His guilt consumed him. He had never lied to her, never hidden anything from her, but now he was keeping his sorrow to himself. He couldn't bear to see her worried, not when he was the cause of her pain.

One evening, as his mother sat on the couch, silently folding clothes, KK walked over to her. He didn't say a word;

he simply sat beside her, placed his head in her lap, and let the tears that he had held in for so long now flow freely.

"Mum," he whispered, his voice thick with emotion. "I am sorry... Because of me, you have tears in your eyes."

His mother's hand trembled as she gently caressed his head. She didn't speak right away, but her touch was enough to break him completely. After a long silence, she finally spoke, her voice soft but filled with love.

"I'm worried for you, Beta," she said, her voice breaking. "No matter what this world does to you, I shall always love you."

The tears came harder now, and KK couldn't stop them. For the first time in years, he allowed himself to be vulnerable. He had spent so long pretending to be strong, but now, in his mother's embrace, he could finally let go.

"Beta," his mother continued, "I have one wish. Will you help me fulfill it?"

KK, his heart heavy with guilt, looked up at her. He already knew what she would ask. She had been waiting for this moment. But he couldn't refuse her. Not after everything.

"Maa," he whispered, his voice hoarse. "I will do whatever you feel is best for me."

His mother, her face lighting up with surprise and joy, immediately hugged him tightly. "Thank you, Beta," she whispered. "Trust me, I will get the most beautiful girl for you, the one who will care for you."

And so, the search began.

Over the next few weeks, KK's family communicated the decision to the relatives, who began scouring the matrimonial site for a suitable match for KK. His brother and sister spent hours online, finding potential matches, but it was always the same story—rejection because of his looks. Time and time again, KK's family faced rejection after rejection. They tried, but nothing worked.

KK, ever the silent observer, didn't intervene. He had already resigned himself to the fact that love was never meant for him. He had become numb to it; he was just going through the motions. His family, however, was determined. They continued the search, even though the results never changed.

One day, a new match appeared on the site—a girl named Khushi, from Uttarakhand. She had accepted his proposal. Her pictures were stunning, her smile radiated warmth, and there was something about her name that seemed to promise hope. Khushi, like many before her, was beautiful—far too beautiful, KK thought.

KK hesitated at first, unsure if he could bear another heartbreak, but her persistence caught his attention. Her messages kept coming, each one more caring than the last. Finally, he responded, sharing his contact number.

The first conversation was brief, but they learned they worked at the same organization in different locations and lived within a few kilometers of each other. KK didn't expect much, but as the days passed, they continued to exchange messages.

However, there were two obstacles—horoscope matching and Khushi's age as she was a year older than him. His family, being traditional, insisted on checking the stars. The astrologer's verdict was not in their favor. The horoscopes didn't match. Khushi was a Manglik, a condition that could bring misfortune.

KK smiled when his mother shared the news with him. "It's okay, Mom," he said, "I'm used to it."

He then spoke to Khushi, gently telling her about the mismatch. Khushi, ever graceful, accepted the situation with understanding. "It's alright, KK," she replied. "We can still be friends." They agreed to remain friends, but their connection was far from over.

They continued to talk, and soon they made plans to meet. The first meeting was at Rajiv Chowk Metro Station, where they would both take the metro to their respective offices. KK arrived early, not wanting to keep her waiting. When Khushi arrived, KK was taken aback by her beauty. She was shorter than he had imagined, but her presence was intoxicating. Her beauty, radiant and pure, had a glow that captivated him. She was graceful, her smile, like sunlight, broke through the clouds.

Her eyes, like dawn, light up the skies,
A soft glow dances where beauty lies.
Her smile, a melody, pure and true,
In her presence, the world feels new.

They walked to a nearby café and ordered cappuccinos, the conversation flowing effortlessly between them. They laughed, shared stories, and enjoyed each other's company. For the first time in a long while, KK felt the weight of the world lift from his shoulders.

For a brief moment, KK forgot about his pain. He forgot about the years of rejection. He forgot about the face he hated so much. All he could see was her—Khushi, a girl with a heart as beautiful as her smile.

But as they bid goodbye, both heading to their respective offices, there was a lingering question in KK's heart. Could this be something real? Or was he destined to be alone forever?

For now, the answer remained unclear. But in that fleeting moment, KK allowed himself to feel something: hope.

* * * * *

Chapter 17

Another Leap of Faith

Over the past few months, KK and Khushi had grown closer, yet their connection remained grounded in the simplicity of friendship. They met at their favorite coffee shop in Rajiv Chowk Metro Station, a place where the world seemed to pause for them, despite the chaos around. It was here, amidst the hum of commuters and the aroma of freshly brewed coffee, that they found solace in each other's company.

For KK, these meetings meant more than casual chats about work and life. With each passing conversation, he found himself drawn to Khushi—not just for her talkative nature, which brought joy into every moment, but also for the warmth in her smile that made his world feel a little brighter. She was the youngest in her family, and her stories about growing up in a joint family touched KK's heart. She spoke of her mother, who had passed away due to cancer. Khushi's voice trembled as she shared how the illness had been diagnosed only in its final stages. "It felt like time slipped away from us too quickly," she said softly one evening.

Khushi also talked about her life with her extended family—her elder brother, who was married; and her two elder sisters, each with children of their own. She lived with her *chacha* and *chachi*, who had two boys younger than her. KK listened to her with an open heart, trying to understand her world, even though his own world was filled with complexities. She was a beacon of light for him, yet he couldn't shake the feeling that his past and the realities of life would make any future with her impossible.

One evening, after their usual coffee meeting, KK's phone buzzed with a call from Khushi's elder brother, Chirag.

"KK, we know you and Khushi have been meeting regularly," Chirag said, his tone casual but probing. "What should we take this as? Are we moving forward with the marriage proposal?"

KK's response was swift, but his heart raced. "We're just friends. And besides, you know our horoscopes don't match. It's not going to work."

Chirag sighed, but his voice remained calm. "Do you really believe in horoscopes? A successful marriage is built on friendship, and Khushi speaks very highly of you. Think about it, KK. Sometimes, life gives us chances that go beyond the stars."

A few days later, KK met Khushi at their usual spot. His mind was clouded with the conversation he'd had with Chirag. He needed to speak to her, to clear the air.

"Khushi," KK began, his voice quieter than usual, "Your brother called me. He wants to know if we're moving ahead with the marriage proposal. But I've told him we're just friends."

Khushi looked at him, a soft smile playing on her lips. "I know," she replied, her voice steady. "We never agreed to it. But I like you, KK. You're a wonderful person, and you're an even better friend."

KK's heart ached at her words. "But Khushi, you know our horoscopes don't match. My family will never accept it. It's not going to happen. And you don't know everything about me..."

Khushi tilted her head, her eyes softening. "Really, KK? Then tell me about yourself. Today, I'll listen."

For the first time, KK felt the weight of his past lift as he began to speak. He told her about the heartbreaks that had scarred him over the years and his past relationships, each more painful than the last, that had molded him into someone impulsive, quick-tempered, and often distant. He confessed that he had developed a habit of smoking heavily, a way to numb the pain that never seemed to subside.

"I never wanted to get married, Khushi," he said, his voice low. "But my mother... my mother wants me to consider it. That's the only reason I'm even open to the idea."

Khushi listened, her heart heavy with empathy. When he finished speaking, she gently placed her hand on his. Her eyes glistened with unshed tears, but she smiled softly.

"You know, KK, most people spend their lives chasing diamonds but throw them away when they think they're just pieces of coal. You've been through so much, but your heart... your heart is a diamond, even if you can't see it. I don't care about your past because the past is something we can't control. What matters is who you are now—and I believe you have a heart that could never hurt anyone, not even in your wildest dreams."

KK was speechless. He felt like he had been hit by a wave of warmth. It hit him deeply, and for a moment, he questioned everything he had believed in. But still, he hesitated. "I don't know, Khushi. You don't know everything about me."

Khushi smiled, her innocence shining through. "I don't need to. What matters is that I like you for who you are. And I'm willing to try."

Before they left for the office, Khushi, with a playful twinkle in her eye, asked, "Should I have my brother speak to your family?"

KK hesitated but then said, "Do what you think is right."

As the days passed, KK's family remained firm in their decision. Despite their own reservations about Khushi being Manglik and the horoscope mismatch, Khushi's elder brother, Chirag, continued to push for the idea.

"I know your family won't agree, but maybe you can make a difference. Khushi likes you a lot, KK. She wants to spend her life with you," Chirag said during a call.

KK remained cold, his heart guarded. "Even though I like her as a friend, I can't go against my family's wishes. It's just not possible."

Chirag gave him time to think. "I understand, but if you change your mind, let us know. You two are a great match, and I'm sure we can work out the Manglik issue. Your consent matters more than anything now."

That evening, KK's mother approached him, her heart full of worry.

She had seen the way her son had withdrawn into himself, how he had lost his spark.

"Beta, what's bothering you?" she asked softly.

KK looked up at her, his eyes filled with a mixture of sadness and resignation. "Maa, you know the astrologers said it wouldn't work. Khushi's family is pressurizing me to share my verdict on the same."

His mother sat beside him, her voice filled with quiet concern. "Do you like her?"

KK nodded slowly. "Yes, but our horoscopes don't match. The astrologer has also said that the marriage will bring nothing but sorrow."

His mother's heart broke for him. She knew the pain he carried, and seeing him so helpless made her want to fight for his happiness.

She went to KK's father, who was reluctant to change his stance. They spoke late into the night, weighing the pros and cons, until KK's mother finally spoke with a resolve that surprised even her. "I can't watch him suffer, even if the stars are against us. I want to see him happy. Let's meet Khushi's family and see if we can make this work."

The next day, KK's father, holding both Khushi's and KK's horoscopes, visited several astrologers, hoping for a solution. But their verdicts were the same—no match. No remedies.

When KK's mother told him the news, he simply smiled faintly. "It's okay, Maa. I expected this."

But deep inside, KK's heart yearned for something more. He knew that sometimes, love can't be decided by stars and horoscopes. It had to come from the heart.

As KK stood on the balcony later that evening, a cigarette between his fingers, the cool night air brushed his face. His thoughts were chaotic, but his heart was clear. He called Chirag and, with a heavy heart, told him the truth: "I've thought it through. It's just not possible."

Chirag wished him the best, but KK couldn't shake the feeling that he had lost something important.

Yet, that night, something inside KK's mother shifted. She couldn't bear to see her son in this state any longer. She stood tall, determined to fight for him. She spoke to KK's father, and after a long night of discussion, they agreed.

The following day, they set up a meeting with Khushi's family. Both families came together, and for the first time, KK felt a sense of hope. The talks were positive, and they discussed the possibility of moving forward.

As the evening drew to a close, both families exchanged smiles, agreeing to move ahead with the engagement and marriage. KK's family made it clear—no dowry. They simply wanted Khushi, not material gifts. The date for the engagement and wedding was finally decided, marking a moment of pure delight and celebration for both families. The news brought smiles, laughter, and an air of anticipation that seemed to envelop everyone. Relatives and friends exchanged congratulatory messages, their hearts brimming with joy as they envisioned the grand union. The elders blessed the couple with prayers for a prosperous future, while the younger ones eagerly began dreaming of festivities, dances, and vibrant ceremonies. Conversations turned to wedding plans, from selecting the perfect venue to designing outfits, as the families united in their shared happiness. It was a time when love and togetherness lit every corner of their lives."

KK realized that sometimes, fate was kinder than the stars in the sky.

Stars may align or drift apart,
But love finds its way through every heart.
In the face of doubt, let trust remain,
For in the end, love is worth the pain.

The journey was far from over, but at that moment, KK knew that no matter what challenges lay ahead, he had finally chosen to take the leap of faith.

* * * * *

Chapter 18

The Wedding Bells!

The sun rose with a golden promise as the countdown to KK and Khushi's new beginning began. Happiness danced through the air, settling in every corner of their homes. KK's family—his mum, dad, brother, sister, brother-in-law, and relatives—had been busy distributing engagement cards for weeks. Khushi's family mirrored the excitement—relatives pouring in, laughter bouncing off the walls, and every corner of the house adorned with flowers, lights, and the aroma of homemade sweets.

Despite the joy, KK's heart held a quiet storm. Memories of his past whispered doubts, but Khushi's radiant presence, her unwavering belief in their love, was his anchor. As the engagement day approached, KK often found himself pausing amidst the chaos, praying silently, "Please let this be my happily ever after."

The days became a blur of activity—shopping trips, fittings, and endless discussions about decor, themes, and rituals. KK and Khushi, now spending more time together, found joy in the smallest things such as picking the perfect shade of flowers, debating over invitation card designs, or simply stealing moments of laughter amidst the chaos.

But life threw them a curveball. The corporate policy at their workplace forbade couples from working together after marriage. With unwavering determination, KK chose to move, prioritizing their future. Miraculously, he landed a position at a prestigious conglomerate, a testament to their shared belief that their love would overcome all odds. “Lady luck,” KK thought, “She’s my blessing in disguise.”

Their journey began with a sacred visit to the Sai temple. Together, KK and Khushi knelt, their hands folded in gratitude. “Whatever comes our way, we’ll face it together,” Khushi whispered, her eyes filled with conviction. KK nodded, her words seeping into his heart, silencing the echoes of his past.

One night during the festivities, KK video-called Khushi and noticed her eyes were wet. “I’m happy,” she said, her voice trembling, “but I miss my Mom.” KK’s heart ached. “She’s watching over you, Khushi,” he said gently. “She’s proud of you, and she’s right here, in your smile.”

The day of engagement finally arrived, a day sparkling with excitement and hope. Khushi’s family had booked a grand banquet hall at a five-star hotel in Delhi. By the time KK’s family reached the venue, it was a sight to behold. The hall was transformed into a paradise of lights, roses, and chandeliers shimmering like stars.

As KK stepped onto the stage, surrounded by friends and relatives, his eyes searched for Khushi. The crowd fell silent as a soulful tune played, and there she was—descending the staircase like a dream. Her pink lehenga glimmered with gold embroidery, every detail accentuating her elegance. Her hair was adorned with jasmine flowers, and her jewelry sparkled like constellations against the night sky.

KK's heart skipped a beat. She was radiant and ethereal—a vision he could barely believe was real. Time seemed to halt as their eyes met, and in that moment, the world around them ceased to exist.

As he slid the diamond ring onto her finger, KK glanced at his mother. Tears glistened in her eyes, a mix of joy and relief as she watched her son finally find happiness. Her tear-filled eyes spoke of joy and relief; her promise to her son was finally fulfilled. Khushi's family cheered as she placed a ring on KK's finger, sealing their bond. The rest of the evening was a whirlwind of laughter, photos, and celebrations. KK's whispered words to Khushi lingered in her heart: "Thank you for being my strength." Her reply, simple yet profound, "That's why I'm marrying you," became their unspoken vow.

With the engagement behind them, the focus shifted to the grand wedding. Both families were on their toes, ensuring every detail was perfect. KK's parents, overwhelmed with happiness, decided to make the wedding a grand affair, inviting everyone, including relatives from their hometown in Himachal Pradesh.

The pre-wedding festivities were a kaleidoscope of joy. The *haldi* ceremony at KK's house was a riot of laughter and music as relatives smeared turmeric on him amidst traditional songs. The *mehndi* night at Khushi's house was equally vibrant, with her cousins and aunts dancing to upbeat Bollywood tracks.

The *sangeet* became the highlight. KK's sister choreographed a performance recounting KK's journey from heartbreak to love, leaving everyone in splits. Meanwhile, Khushi's brother pulled out all the stops with a surprise act, recreating moments from her childhood, bringing tears and laughter in equal measure.

The big day dawned with an air of festivity. KK's morning began with the traditional public bath, where relatives poured water over him amidst songs and laughter. His *sehra bandi* ceremony saw him draped in garlands of currency notes, symbolizing prosperity. By evening, KK was ready to mount the mare for the *ghurchari*.

As the *baraat* made its way to the venue, the sky lit up with fireworks. KK's brother-in-law threw wads of 500 and 1000-rupee notes into the air, adding to the revelry with lots of fireworks as a symbol of celebration and happiness. At the venue gate, Khushi's sisters-in-law blocked their entry, demanding a hefty *sagan*. Amidst laughter and playful negotiations, KK handed over ⊠5001, sealing the deal with a chuckle.

Inside, the hall was a spectacle. Khushi appeared, dressed in a sea-green lehenga that shimmered like dawn's first light. Her jewelry, intricate and regal, complemented her radiant smile. KK's heart raced as she walked toward him, her veil catching the soft glow of chandeliers.

The exchange of garlands was met with cheers and the flash of cameras. They were celebrities for the night, surrounded by love. After the feast, the *pheras* began. As they circled the sacred fire, they made promises to stand by each other through every storm, to nurture their love and their dreams together.

The *bidaai* was bittersweet. Khushi hugged her family tightly, tears streaming as she left her childhood home. But amidst the sorrow was the excitement of beginning a new chapter. KK's mother waited eagerly at their doorstep, singing traditional songs to welcome the new couple.

As KK and Khushi entered their home, hands entwined, their hearts echoed the same silent vow: "This is the beginning of forever."

In her smile, I found my dawn,
In her eyes, my nights are drawn.
Together, we'll weather the storm and sea,
For love, at last, was meant for me.

And as the first rays of sunlight bathed their new home, KK and Khushi knew deep in their hearts that this was not just the start of a new journey, but the beginning of a love story written in the stars, destined to shine forever.

* * * * *

Chapter 19

The Journey of Promises

The wedding festivities had faded, leaving behind a lingering warmth that wrapped KK and Khushi in a cocoon of happiness. The house that once echoed with laughter, blessings, and the rhythmic beats of *dhol* was now quiet as relatives bid their farewells. For KK, this silence wasn't emptiness—it was the calm before a new adventure, the honeymoon to Mauritius, one he had meticulously planned to begin their life together.

The morning of their departure arrived. KK had been up all night, double-checking their tickets, passports, and the itinerary he had so carefully curated. As they drove to the airport, Khushi sat beside him, her eyes sparkling with excitement.

"You're unusually quiet," she said, nudging him gently.

"I'm just thinking," KK replied, his voice soft. "Thinking about how lucky I am to have you in my life."

Khushi blushed, her cheeks turning the color of blooming roses. "And I'm lucky to have you."

Their flight took off, carrying with it KK's dreams of giving Khushi the perfect start to their married life. As the plane soared through the clouds, Khushi looked out of the window, her childlike wonder bringing a smile to KK's face.

As they landed in Mauritius, the warmth of the tropical air greeted them, carrying with it the scent of saltwater and blooming frangipani. Their resort was a haven of luxury, nestled amidst swaying palm trees and overlooking a serene, turquoise lagoon.

"KK, this is beautiful!" Khushi exclaimed as they entered their suite. The room was adorned with petals of red and white roses, the bed draped in soft linens, and the balcony offered a view of the endless ocean.

KK held her hand and said, "This is just the beginning, Khushi. I want to give you the world."

In your eyes, I see my dreams unfold,
In your laughter, warmth sweeter than gold.
With every moment, a promise I renew,
To give the world and the stars to you.

Their days in Mauritius were a blend of adventure and romance. One morning, KK surprised Khushi with a snorkeling trip at Blue Bay Marine Park. As they floated in the crystal-clear waters, Khushi hesitated, clutching KK's arm tightly.

"What if I can't do it?" she whispered.

"You can and you will," KK assured her. "I'm right here with you."

Khushi's initial fear dissolved into awe as she gazed at the underwater world—vibrant coral reefs, schools of rainbow-colored fish, and the silent rhythm of the ocean. She emerged from the water, her face glowing with joy.

"This is amazing!" she said, hugging KK. "Thank you for pushing me to try."

Evenings were their favorite time. The sun would set, painting the sky in shades of orange and purple, and they would sit on the beach, sharing dreams and whispered secrets. One evening, KK arranged a candlelit dinner on a private yacht. As the gentle waves rocked the boat, they toasted to their new life.

"What do you see in our future, KK?" Khushi asked, her voice filled with curiosity.

"A life full of love, laughter, and memories like this," he replied, his eyes locking with hers.

Their final night in Mauritius was magical. Under a sky adorned with stars, KK knelt on one knee—not with a ring, but with words.

"Khushi," he began, "this trip has been the happiest time of my life. I promise to keep this happiness alive, no matter what comes our way."

Khushi's eyes filled with tears. "And I promise to be your strength, always," she said.

Their return to India didn't dim the glow of their honeymoon; if anything, it strengthened their bond. KK and Khushi were inseparable, their love growing with each passing day. KK often marveled at how effortlessly Khushi had become the center of his universe.

Months turned into seasons, and one fine evening, Khushi came to KK with a twinkle in her eye.

"I have something to tell you," she said, her voice trembling with excitement.

"What is it, Khushi?" KK asked, sensing her joy.

"We're going to be parents!" she exclaimed, tears streaming down her face.

KK froze for a moment, the weight of her words sinking in. Then, overwhelmed with emotion, he pulled her into a tight embrace.

"I can't believe it," he whispered. "This is the happiest day of my life."

In your womb, a miracle takes flight,
A tiny heartbeat, a spark of light.
Our love now blooms in this divine gift,
A part of you, a part of mine.

The news brought immense joy to their families. KK's mother was overjoyed, her eyes glistening with tears as she hugged her son.

"Khushi has given us the greatest blessing," she said, her voice choked with emotion.

From that day on, KK became a doting husband. He attended every doctor's appointment, researched parenting tips, and ensured Khushi's cravings were always fulfilled. He even took leave from work whenever she needed extra care.

"You're spoiling me," Khushi teased one day as KK brought her a plate of mangoes and pickles.

"You deserve to be spoiled," he replied with a smile.

The day finally arrived—6th September 2013. Khushi went into labor in the early hours of the morning, and KK was a bundle of nerves. As he paced the hospital corridor, his thoughts oscillated between excitement and fear.

"Please let everything go well," he silently prayed, clutching the small Saibaba locket around his neck.

Hours later, the doctor emerged with a wide smile. "Congratulations, Mr. KK! It's a boy!"

KK rushed into the room, his eyes welling up as he saw Khushi holding their newborn son. The tiny bundle of joy had a tuft of black hair and a cry that filled the room with life.

"He's beautiful," KK whispered, his voice trembling.

Khushi smiled weakly. "We did it, KK."

The family welcomed the baby with open arms, organizing a grand naming ceremony. KK's parents suggested the name Inesh, meaning King of Kings.

A king is born, a light divine,
A little hand now holding mine.
In his smile, I see my skies,
A love eternal, that never dies.

Life became a beautiful chaos. Inesh brought endless joy to their home, even as sleepless nights became the norm. KK would often stay awake, rocking Inesh to sleep while humming lullabies.

"Why don't you rest?" his mother would ask.

"I can't get enough of him," KK would reply with a smile.

Though life wasn't always easy, KK cherished every moment. Inesh's laughter became his greatest reward, and Khushi's presence remained his anchor. As he looked at his growing family, KK felt a sense of fulfillment that words could never capture.

But little did he know, the fairytale would soon face challenges that would test the strength of his love and resolve.

* * * * *

Chapter 20

The Unseen Storm

Fairy tales often mask the undercurrents of reality. As Khushi recovered and resumed work, her behavior began to shift. She grew distant, avoiding both KK and Inesh. The warmth that once radiated from her seemed to fade, replaced by indifference.

"I never wanted a child so early," she confessed one day, leaving KK stunned. This had been a mutual decision—one they had celebrated together. Her words pierced his heart, yet he chose to focus on the laughter of his son rather than the growing silence between him and Khushi.

In the early days of their marriage, Khushi was warm, caring, and full of life. But slowly, over the years, her love seemed to fade. The spark that once lit her eyes dimmed into a flickering candle, struggling against the wind.

In the echoes of silence, he stood alone,
A father's heart, a lover's tone.
In her absence, his soul did ache,
A bond of love, beginning to break.

By 2020, eight years of marriage had passed, and with it, the sparkle of love had dimmed between

KK and Khushi. KK had done everything he could to make her happy—from loving her passionately to buying jewelry, planning surprise trips, and celebrating her birthday and their anniversaries in grand style. He did it all, but despite his efforts, Khushi remained distant, unappreciative, and detached. No matter what he did, no matter how hard he tried, the woman he adored had become a stranger.

As the pandemic hit, her distance from him had grown unbearable. COVID-19 arrived like a storm in 2020, and while the world shut down, the tension at home intensified. KK had always been cautious about his family's safety. He urged Khushi to work from home, especially due to his aging parents and Inesh being just a child. But Khushi resisted. She still wanted to go to the office. Her pride and ambition mattered more to her than the well-being of the family. KK, despite the obvious risks, relented. He continued to work from home and did everything he could to ensure their parents and Inesh were safe.

When the lockdowns became mandatory, Khushi's company still refused to let her work from home, denying her a laptop. The moment the government ordered work from home, KK didn't hesitate; he bought her a laptop, hoping she'd settle in. But instead of spending time with the family, Khushi buried herself in the digital world, ignoring Inesh and KK. Her coldness continued to grow, and KK felt himself slowly unraveling.

KK was the one who became Inesh's anchor during those difficult months. He helped his son with schoolwork, kept him entertained, and most importantly, he listened to him. Inesh, always a sharp child, not only excelled academically but also shone in extracurricular activities. He had developed an interest in modeling, and acting, and by the time he was in his teens, he had already made a name for himself in music videos and short films. The boy who could light up any room with his laughter was thriving, despite the neglect from the one person who should have been nurturing him.

KK felt pride in his son, a love so deep that it often overwhelmed him. Inesh's smile was the only thing that made his heart feel whole. But it was becoming increasingly clear to KK that Khushi wasn't there emotionally or mentally. She was somewhere else, in a world far removed from the warmth of the family.

Then, the worst happened. As if the universe was testing KK's limits, his worst fear came true: his parents tested positive for COVID-19. Panic gripped his heart as he rushed to tend to them. But Khushi, as usual, remained distant. While KK and his brother were striving to save their parents from the grips of the virus, Khushi seemed unfazed by the growing danger around them.

When Inesh also tested positive, it was like KK had been struck by lightning. He had done everything to protect his family, and yet, the storm had found its way into their home. The thought of losing his son shattered him completely. KK spent hours on his knees, praying in front of his Saibaba idol. His heart bled for Inesh. "What if I lose him?" was a question that haunted him day and night.

Despite Khushi's coldness, KK never let his fear show. He took care of the house, cared for Inesh, and prayed for his recovery. His heart could not fathom a world where Inesh wasn't by his side. But Khushi, in her usual manner, showed little concern for the situation. She lay in bed, her eyes vacant, while KK did everything—cleaning, cooking, and managing everything.

KK spent sleepless nights by Inesh's side, watching his son fight the virus with all the strength he had. He prayed every day, hoping for a miracle. And slowly, the miracle came. The family recovered, but the wounds remained.

With the worst behind them, KK insisted that the family, including his parents, should leave for Himachal Pradesh to avoid any more risks. Khushi refused, citing the need to return to the office. As always, she put her career above everything. So, KK, with Inesh in tow, remained behind in Delhi.

While KK's family recovered and traveled to Himachal for a much-needed break, Khushi's neglect of their son only deepened. The house became a mess—clothes piling up, the beds unmade, and dust accumulating. When KK confronted her, hoping for some change, the walls that had grown between them seemed only taller. Their arguments became more frequent, but nothing ever changed.

It was one particular evening, though, that broke something inside KK. He walked into the kitchen to find Inesh being served a plate of food—dal with beetle cooked in it, the stench unbearable. He tried to remain calm, but the anger built up in him. He turned to Khushi and demanded an explanation. She offered none, only a cold, indifferent apology that felt hollow. But when, on another day, he found a worm crawling in the dates Khushi had served to Inesh, something inside KK snapped. How could she do this to their child? How could she be so careless, so cold?

"Why are you doing this, Khushi? Why are you hurting me?"

KK's voice trembled with the pain of his realization. He had loved her deeply, but she seemed to have become someone else. Someone unrecognizable. Khushi's response was dismissive, as always. She claimed it was an accident. But how many accidents could a mother have? KK's patience was at its limit.

He had been patient, hopeful, loving, and understanding. But all his efforts had amounted to nothing. His heart was breaking for his son, for the life he had once dreamed of. The woman he had loved had become his greatest sorrow.

Then, the unthinkable happened. Khushi contracted COVID herself. Her body was weak, her breath shallow. KK, despite the anger and resentment that had built up over the years, did what any devoted husband would do. He took care of her, isolated her in a room to keep Inesh safe, and tended to her as if she were the most important person in his life. He cooked for her, cleaned the house, and prayed for her recovery. His love for her never faltered, even in the face of all her neglect. His only solace was his belief in Saibaba, who had always guided him through the darkest times.

Khushi's condition worsened. She became feverish and delirious. But KK never left her side. He spent sleepless nights praying, hoping, and doing everything he could. And slowly, like a candle flickering back to life, she recovered. It wasn't love that had been restored, but a sense of duty. Khushi's return to health was a relief, but it wasn't the salvation of their marriage that KK had hoped for.

He gave his all, his love, his soul,
Yet the void grew, an empty hole.
A love he cherished, slipping away,
What lies ahead, who's to say?

As soon as Khushi recovered and COVID was also in control, KK suggested they take a trip—away from the pressures of daily life, to rediscover the joy they once shared. The trip was filled with moments of tenderness, but as soon as they returned home, the old patterns resurfaced.

Khushi was back to being distant, aloof, and indifferent. KK realized that no matter how hard he tried, things weren't going to change. He had reached the breaking point.

In a moment of clarity, KK knew he had to seek counsel from her family. But the decision weighed heavily on him. He had never imagined a life without Khushi, yet their love seemed to be a memory, a broken picture hanging on the wall of their past.

A home once filled with untold dreams,
Now standing in silence, stark and cold.
In the ashes of love, a question burned,
Is this the end, or a lesson learned?

* * * * *

Chapter 21

The Crack Begins to Appear

KK sat in the dimly lit room, his fingers trembling as he clasped the photo frame in his hands. It was a picture of them, him and Khushi, smiling at their wedding, their eyes full of promises they once made. He stared at it, unable to recognize the woman in the photo anymore. Where had she gone? The woman who once held his hand in the darkest of times, the woman who laughed with him through their struggles, the woman who promised to be his forever? Now, she was a ghost in his life, drifting farther away with every passing day.

The house had grown quieter and emptier, the walls echoing the sound of his loneliness. His heart ached, not just because of the silence, but because the one person who once filled it with love was now the cause of his deepest sorrow.

He had tried. Oh, how he had tried! He had tried to love her even when she seemed distant, even when her eyes no longer sparkled with the same warmth. He had tried to hold onto the woman he had fallen in love with, but she was slipping through his fingers with every passing day, and there was nothing he could do to stop it.

The night was always the hardest. As he lay on the bed, Inesh snuggled against him, he would look at the empty space beside him where Khushi once slept. The void was a cold, unforgiving place.

"How did it come to this, Khushi?
How did we lose ourselves in the dance of time?
I gave you my heart, I gave you my soul,
But now I'm left with just a hollow rhyme."

Every word felt like a dagger to his heart, but he couldn't stop the flow of emotions. He had loved her deeply, with a sincerity that could move mountains, yet it seemed to count for nothing now. The distance between them had become insurmountable, and he didn't know if he had the strength to climb it anymore.

It had been a month since they had stopped talking, and KK had decided to confront the issue. The truth burned in his heart, but he had no other choice but to speak it.

The night before, as KK lay in bed, staring at the ceiling, a thought struck him. Is this it? He wondered. Is this the end of our story? And then, sleep began to overtake him as he planned to speak to her family, to open up about the toll his marriage was taking on him.

The next morning, he called Chirag, the one person who could understand the depth of his turmoil.

"Chirag..." His voice faltered as he spoke. "Khushi... she's changed. I don't know what happened, but she doesn't care about me anymore. She doesn't care about Inesh. She's always distant, lost in her own world. I don't know what to do."

Chirag, who had always been the calm one in the family, listened patiently. But his response wasn't what KK had hoped for.

"KK, life changes when you have a kid. You have to understand that Khushi is probably overwhelmed. She's trying to balance everything, and you need to make more effort," Chirag said, his voice calm but distant. "You just need to give her time."

KK's breath caught in his chest. Time? Was that really what it was? Time? He had been waiting for her for years now, for any sign of the woman he had once known, but it was like waiting for rain in a drought.

"I've been giving her time, Chirag," KK replied, his voice breaking. "But she's not the same. She doesn't care about me, or about Inesh. She's drifting farther away, and I feel powerless to stop it. I don't even recognize the woman I married."

Chirag, always the one to side with family, offered his usual response. "KK, you need to make more of an effort. Maybe she's just adjusting to everything, to the changes in her life."

KK clenched his fists. He wanted to scream, to tell Chirag that he had tried, that he had given everything to make things work, but the words stuck in his throat. He was alone in this fight, and it felt like no one truly understood the depth of his pain. He was drowning in his own emotions, but no one saw it. No one understood the weight of carrying a love that had turned into a burden.

"You're not the problem, but sometimes we have to understand what the other person is going through," Chirag said. He further added that he would try to speak to her.

A few days later, Khushi did show small signs of change. She spent more time with Inesh, and for a fleeting moment, KK thought things might get better. He clung to that hope, telling himself that as long as she was giving their son the love he deserved, he could bear the rest. But the change was short-lived. As the months passed, the distance between them became more palpable. Khushi's absence was suffocating, her indifference even more so.

The house had turned into a place of silence, of unspoken words. They had stopped eating together. Khushi came home late. KK, tired from work and the constant strain of holding everything together, tried to be patient. He tried to wait for her, to hold onto the belief that things would get better.

But it was hard when it felt like she was slipping away with every passing day.

One evening, KK was caught off guard. He had been feeling unwell, his back aching from his cervical spondylosis, and his body fighting the allergies that had plagued him for weeks. He was lying on the couch when he picked up Khushi's phone, needing to check the parents' group messages. His phone was charging, and hers was lying next to him.

The screen lit up with a message that made his heart stop.

"I am thankful to have you in my life and I love you."

It wasn't from Khushi. It was from someone he didn't know. The profile picture showed a female, but there was no mistaking it. The message was meant for Khushi.

His breath caught in his throat. The room seemed to spin. Was this what he thought it was? Was Khushi in love with someone else? He didn't want to believe it. He couldn't.

When Khushi came in, KK couldn't hold it in any longer. His voice cracked as he asked, "Khushi, what's going on? Who is she?"

Her face flushed with anger, and she snapped, "How dare you look at my private messages!"

"I was just checking the group for updates," KK said, his heart racing. "But who is this person?"

"Stick to your own phone, and yes, she's an old friend of mine!" Khushi snapped, her words sharp like a blade.

KK felt his world collapsing around him. The walls he had built for their love were crumbling, and he had no idea how to stop it. He didn't care about her having friends, but the message, the love, the words she had shared with someone else—it hurt more than he could ever explain.

His voice faltered as he asked, "Are you straight with me, Khushi? Is there something you're not telling me?"

Her eyes narrowed, fury burning in them. "How dare you ask me that? You have no right to invade my privacy! Stay out of my business!"

The argument spiraled out of control and words were thrown like knives, each one cutting deeper than the last. KK's mind raced, but the only thing he could focus on was the pain in his chest. The love he had given her had turned into something unrecognizable. The woman he had married, the one he had trusted with his heart, was slipping away, piece by piece.

"I never touched you, Khushi! I never hurt you!" KK shouted, his voice raw with emotion.

But Khushi, her face a mask of anger, turned away. "You're suffocating me, KK. I need space."

"Please, Khushi, don't leave. Not like this. Not after everything we've been through," he begged, his voice cracking.

But she didn't listen. She grabbed her phone and walked out of the bedroom to another room in the house, leaving KK standing there with nothing but a broken heart and a shattered soul. Inesh, confused and scared, clung to his father, unaware of the storm that had just torn their world apart.

The days that followed were a blur of pain. Khushi came home late from her usual time every night, distant and cold. Dinner was always ordered in, and KK didn't know how to fix what had been broken. He felt like he was losing her, piece by piece, but there was nothing he could do to stop it.

One night, when Khushi was late again, KK tried to reach her. He called, but her phone went straight to voicemail. Inesh tried calling too, but there was no answer. The worry began to consume him. He had no idea where she was, and with each passing minute, his fear grew.

His calls to her boss went unanswered, and panic set in. He called her from his mother's phone. When Khushi's father picked up the phone, KK's world crumbled.

"Papa, have you seen Khushi? She hasn't come home yet,"

"She's with me," Khushi's father replied coldly. "She's not coming back after what happened last night."

"What are you talking about? I never hurt her, never laid a hand on her!" KK shouted, his voice desperate.

"You beat her, KK," Khushi's father said. "You abused her, and she's at the police station right now. They'll be calling you soon."

KK's heart stopped. His whole body went numb. The accusation was too much to bear. He had been accused of something he hadn't done, something he could never do. And now, his own family was turning against him.

At the police station, the truth was twisted, and KK found himself in the middle of a nightmare he couldn't escape. Khushi, refusing a medical check-up, stood by her false claims. Inesh, the only innocent soul in the room, told the truth, but Khushi dismissed him, accusing them both of lying.

And then, in the cold, sterile atmosphere of the station, Khushi left him. She walked out with her father, leaving KK and Inesh shattered and broken.

"Was this really the end?" he thought as he stood there watching her walk away.

Had he loved too much? Was this the price he had to pay for loving her unconditionally?

I gave you my heart, but you tore it apart.
I waited in silence while you danced in the dark.
You were my soul, my everything,
Now you're a ghost that I can't even cling.

The question echoed in his mind, but he knew one thing for certain: he had lost her.

* * * * *

Chapter 22

The Ashes of Love

The world had taken a sudden, cruel U-turn for KK, as Khushi, the woman he had once adored, decided to him and Inesh forever. In an instant, everything felt like it was slipping through his fingers. It was as if the universe itself had conspired to break him. KK had always believed in the balance of life—You cannot clap with one hand. But now, as Khushi turned away, he found himself clutching onto the fragments of a dream, blaming himself for everything that had gone wrong. What had he missed? What had he done wrong? But there was nothing he could change. The past was always a past—irreparable.

"Did I fail you, Khushi? Was my love not enough to keep us whole?"

Even after coming back home from the police station, when every ounce of his strength had been drained, he tried reaching out to her. The phone calls went unanswered, and eventually, he was blocked. Khushi had made her decision, and the heartache that followed was unbearable. That night, KK wept. His tears blurred his vision, but the soft voice of his son, Inesh, brought him back to reality.

In the shadow of despair, where the heart feels alone,
A tiny hand reached out, a love unknown.
Inesh, my beacon in the darkest of night,
Your pure, innocent love became my guiding light.

The little boy, just nine years old, stood by his father, his pure, innocent eyes looking at him with unwavering love.

"Papa, don't cry," Inesh said, holding his father's hand firmly. "I will never leave you." And for a brief moment, that promise was enough to give KK the strength to carry on, even though his world was breaking apart.

KK never wanted to part with Khushi, not under any circumstances.

Despite all that had happened, he made several attempts to bring her back. He visited her father's house, but each time, he was humiliated and that too in front of Inesh. Each rejection, each insult, chipped away at his spirit. The little boy could see his father's pain and told him, "Papa, please stop going there. She doesn't want to come back." The words cut deep, but KK knew his son was right. It was the hardest thing he had ever heard, and it broke him.

Sometimes, the hardest truths are spoken by the smallest voices,
A child's wisdom, silencing the noise of hopeless choices.

Inesh, my anchor, in this storm I'm tossed,
Through your eyes, I find what I thought was lost.

Khushi's family filled her ears with bitterness, and soon enough, Khushi moved forward with litigation. There were no more words left to say; only legal documents and battles awaited. Chirag, her brother, filed a complaint with the National Women's Commission. Khushi, driven by her own anger and ego, took everything a step further, filing complaints for child custody, domestic violence, Section 498A, and even divorce. Not only this, she demanded alimony of one crore and a lakh for maintenance every month. It seemed there was no limit to the damage she wanted to cause.

You walked away, leaving love to die,
With a child, allegations and claims, you made me cry.
Alimony and compensation you ask, while trust is torn,
A battle for peace, in silence I mourn

In the middle of all this chaos, KK never spoke a bad word about her. And every time KK went to court, the feeling of abandonment gnawed at him. Not only was he fighting for his own dignity, but he was also fighting for Inesh's right to have a mother, a right that Khushi had denied him. The legal battles, the manipulations, the endless accusations—it was a war that Khushi waged not just against him, but against the very love they once shared. Yet, her ego had become a wall too high to scale. No reconciliation was possible.

Khushi's neglect of Inesh soon became a part of their daily reality. On weekends, when KK would take Inesh to the park or the movies, he would see other children with their mothers. Inesh would look at them with wide eyes, longing for something he didn't understand. KK would feel the lump in his throat grow with each passing moment, helpless to give Inesh what he needed most—a mother who cared.

In every tear you shed, I see my own pain,
But in your smile, my hope blooms again.
Inesh, my son, you're the love I defend,
In this cruel, fleeting world, you're my forever friend.

And yet, as he watched his son grow more and more distant from her, KK realized the bitter truth. Khushi wasn't going to change. She wasn't going to be the woman he had once loved, and she certainly wasn't going to be the mother that Inesh deserved.

Inesh's innocence was slowly replaced with confusion, and his joy was overshadowed by a sadness he couldn't comprehend. He would still ask about his mother, hoping that one day, she would come back and everything would be like it used to be. But every time, the answer was the same. She wasn't coming back.

"Papa, why doesn't Mama call me?" Inesh asked one evening, his small face crinkled with the weight of a question too heavy for his tender age.

KK held him close, his voice breaking as he whispered, "She has her reasons, Beta. But no matter what happens, Papa will always be here for you. You are my world."

But even as he said those words, KK knew they weren't enough. They would never be enough. How could he explain to his son? How could he protect Inesh from the pain that came with such abandonment? The answer was simple: he couldn't.

KK's mother, once so fond of Khushi, tried reaching out several times, hoping that her daughter-in-law might soften and reconcile with her son. But Khushi refused to respond. She didn't even acknowledge her in-laws' existence anymore. To her, they were just part of the 'enemy' that she was so determined to destroy.

At the same time, life hadn't finished tormenting KK yet. As if he didn't have enough to bear, his boss at work, already aware of the personal turmoil KK was going through, began making his life even more difficult. His personal struggles were shared openly in the office, and soon, KK was humiliated and forced to resign. He pleaded for his salary during the notice period, but his boss refused to listen.

Once again, KK found himself trapped. The weight of his failing marriage, the constant legal battles, the loss of his job—all seemed too much. But he did what he had always done: he fought. He filed litigation against his boss. He reached out to his friend, Deepankur, who was now the founder of a start-up. He offered him a job. It was a huge salary cut, but it was something. It meant he could still provide for Inesh. It meant he could stay in Delhi, where his parents could help him take care of his son while he fought the endless court cases. Deepankur stood by his friend as always and gave all the time he needed to get over the litigations against him.

Yet, Khushi never once asked about Inesh. Not once did she call to check on her son. She had completely distanced herself and was lost in her own world of ego and pride. Her focus now was only on winning her cases, no matter the cost. For her, the battle was no longer about love —it was about revenge. She wanted to take Inesh from KK, and she would stop at nothing to break him, to destroy his very soul.

We sit in shadows, side by side,
A father's grief, a son's denied.
Her love, a ghost we can't erase,
We search for light in this endless space.

The year dragged on. The legal battles wore KK down, but he fought with everything he had. His only reason to keep going was Inesh. Every day, he would fight for his son's future because Inesh was all that KK had left. He was his lifeline, his reason to smile, his reason to breathe.

Despite all the hardships, KK found solace in the unexpected. Amit Thakur and Akash Vajpai, two lawyers, came into his life like his saviors. Both of them believed in him, and together, they stood strong against the tide of false accusations Khushi had hurled at him. Amit and Akash, both kind and humble, were like brothers to KK. They shielded KK from the worst, ensuring that the cases did not progress further.

Khushi's ego continued to swell, and her heart grew colder with every passing moment. After two years of a legal battle, realizing that victory was slipping out of reach, she proposed a mutual divorce, but with a condition so harsh it revealed her indifference—Inesh must remain with his father. Her actions spoke volumes: she had no regard for her son, no regard for the family they had built together. Winning was all that mattered to her.

In her quest for dominance, she took everything KK had carefully saved for Inesh's future. The situation was such that KK had to withdraw money even from his Provident Fund, the dreams he had nurtured for his son's security and happiness. And yet, she refused to contribute even a single penny toward his well-being, turning her back on the very child who deserved her love the most.

The divorce was finalized, just two days before their 12th wedding anniversary. For Khushi, it was a moment of triumph, of finality. But for KK, it was yet another heartbreak. As he stared at the divorce decree, his heart shattered. He still had the door open for Khushi if she ever felt like returning back home, she would be welcome. But through the darkness, one constant remained: Inesh. The boy's laughter, his questions, and his unwavering love became KK's sanctuary.

Though the storm may rage and the skies may fall,
Your love, my son, will conquer it all.
Inesh, my light, in your heart, I see,
The strength to rebuild, the courage to be free.

In the days that followed, KK became a shadow of his former self. The pain was unbearable. His soul felt empty and hollow. "Why me?" he asked God. "Why did I have to endure this?" The man who once believed in love, in family, in togetherness, now found himself alone, his dreams shattered.

He sought solace in cigarettes, the smoke filling the emptiness in his chest, but even that couldn't numb the pain. The love he had given so freely had been tossed aside like nothing more than a forgotten memory. And still, KK fought. For Inesh. For the future. For the love that he had once known.

The world had taken everything from him. But he still had hope. He still had his son. And no matter what, he would fight for him.

As the smoke of his cigarette curled into the air, KK looked at the sky, tears slipping down his face. He knew that love, the kind he had once believed in, had torn him apart. But the love he had for his son? That would never break. And no matter how hard life pushed him, he would never give up on that. Inesh was the reason he would keep going, even if the world itself had crumbled around him.

In the ruins of love, I found a new start,
Through the eyes of my child, the beat of my heart.
Inesh, my forever, my beacon of light,
With you by my side, every shadow takes flight.

KK kissed his son's forehead and whispered, "You are my world, Inesh. You're the reason I'll keep fighting, no matter what."

And with that promise, KK let go of the pain of the past, choosing instead to focus on the love that would never leave him. The love of his son continues to this day. KK still loves Khushi unconditionally and the doors to his heart remain open for her, waiting patiently, like a sanctuary that knows no closure.

Why did they leave a heart in love so torn?
Was it too fragile, or just too worn?
A love once whole, now lost, now cold,
Left to ache, as stories grow old.

"It's not her absence that hurts the most; it's the pieces of her I still see in our child's smile, reminding me of what could have been."

* * * * *

Chapter 23

Through Trials, Friendship Blossoms

The days of loneliness stretched endlessly before KK. The weight of being a single father rested heavily on his shoulders. His heart, once filled with the boundless hopes of love, now lay buried beneath the rubble of broken dreams. Inesh, his son, was the only spark left in his world—a world that had been torn apart by betrayal. KK, though struggling to put his life back together, found solace in the small moments with his son. The giggles, the hand-drawn pictures, the "I love you, Papa" that echoed through their home—they were the glue holding his fractured soul together.

Yet, it wasn't easy. Every day was a battle: between managing a demanding job, keeping up with the endless court dates against his boss, and being a father who could never quite fulfill the role his son deserved. Each night, when Inesh lay asleep, KK would sit by his bedside, his thoughts running wild. Could he really do this on his own? Could he truly give Inesh a happy, stable life without Khushi? The thought often brought a lump to his throat; he would blame himself for all that went wrong, but he knew he had no choice. His past love had failed him, but the love he had for Inesh—his son—was the one thing that would never break.

KK had made peace with one cruel truth: Love was never meant for him. He closed the gates of his heart, bolting them shut with a promise. He would never let anyone close enough to hurt him or Inesh again. Marriage? It was a chapter he had written off entirely, replaced with a solemn vow to devote his life to his son.

It wasn't long before KK's fight with his former employer, who had harassed him and withheld his salary, reached its peak. The court case seemed endless, wearing him down, but in the midst of it, a surprise came in the form of Ruhani, an HR professional at the same organization. Ruhani wasn't just any HR; she was a beacon of justice, a woman of steel who stood up against the wrongs of the world. She had heard about KK's plight and stepped forward as a witness in his case. Her courage and her unwavering belief in fairness struck a chord deep inside him.

With every passing day, Ruhani was there—checking in on the case, asking how things were progressing, and offering both emotional and professional support. KK felt a warmth in her presence, a flicker of hope amidst the storm. He thanked his stars for bringing her into his life, for she was more than just a witness—she had become his angel, quietly supporting him without asking for anything in return.

Ruhani's story was one of strength. A former model and actor who had left her glamorous career to raise her daughter, she understood the complexities of life. And as their bond grew, it became clear to KK that Ruhani was more than just a supporter—she was becoming his closest friend. They joked, they argued, they debated on the finer points of HR processes, but in all of it, there was something deep and genuine. They were like Tom and Jerry—constantly bickering, but always there for each other in the end.

Ruhani became KK's sounding board for everything. As he struggled with the challenges of single parenthood, he began seeking her advice on how to raise Inesh. Ruhani, being a mother herself, shared her wisdom generously. "Sometimes, it's not about being perfect, KK. It's about showing up, loving them with all you've got, and teaching them how to be strong and kind," she would say, and KK would listen intently, soaking in every word.

She taught him the little things that could make all the difference in a child's life—how to listen, how to empathize, and how to never give up on their dreams. KK found himself more confident as a father, realizing that the love he had for Inesh was the foundation of everything. No matter what, he would be there for his son. And through Ruhani's guidance, he was becoming a better man—a man who understood the importance of friendship, of kindness, and of never abandoning the people who truly mattered.

But life wasn't easy for a single father. Balancing the demands of work and home often felt like walking a tightrope. There were mornings when KK would drop little Inesh off at school, his heart heavy with the knowledge that the day ahead would be a whirlwind—rushing to court hearings, juggling back-to-back meetings at the office, and somehow finding time to be the dad he wanted to be. Through it all, KK's mother became a pillar of support. She poured all her love and care into Inesh, just as she had once done for KK, nurturing the boy with the same warmth and devotion. Together, they made sure Inesh never felt the gaps in their world—a testament to their resilience and unconditional love.

Through it all, Ruhani continued to stand by him. She was a constant, a friend who reminded him that even in the darkest times, there was light to be found in the people around him.

Then, the final battle arrived—the case against his former employer. The litigation that had stretched on for far too long was now nearing its end, and with Ruhani's unwavering support, KK finally felt like there was a chance for justice. As the days passed, he kept his fingers crossed, hoping and praying that the truth would prevail.

"Please, God," he whispered during one particularly difficult night, as he sat alone in his room. "Give me the strength to finish this battle, to win for Inesh, to prove that justice can prevail."

With Ruhani's help, he did win. The case was resolved in his favor, and KK's salary was finally released. Justice had been served. At that moment, KK realized that sometimes, life doesn't give you everything you want—but it does give you the strength to keep going.

As the chapter of his life closed with the finality of the litigation, KK smiled at his son, who was fast asleep, his small hands clutching his teddy bear—his dad. He knew that his love for Inesh would never die, no matter how hard the world tried to break him, he would come out stronger than before. And as for love—true love, the kind that nurtures, grows, and stands the test of time—it was found in friendship, in loyalty, in the quiet moments of life.

"Love! It was never meant for me," KK whispered to himself as he gazed out the window. "But I've found something even better. I've found a reason to live, to fight, and to be the father Inesh deserves."

The story of love, loss, and redemption had come full circle. And as the final page turned, KK knew that his journey was far from over as he still awaited the return of Khushi...

"Every time the little fingers wrapped around his hand, it reminded him that love wasn't about what you receive but what you give, endlessly and selflessly."

* * * * *

Chapter 24

Through Their Eyes: Echoes of Love and Madness

Writing this book has been a journey of reflection, healing, and confronting the raw truths of love. While penning down these chapters, KK felt an unshakable pull to look back—not with anger or regret, but with a quiet wish for the well-being of those who had once held pieces of his heart. Despite the heartbreak and the scars, KK believed in the beauty of love, even if it had often been unkind to him.

As part of this journey, KK reached out to his ex-partners, not to rekindle old flames but to hear their truths. To his surprise, many responded, sharing memories, emotions, and their thoughts about him. These are not crafted words from KK's pen but honest reflections from those who had known him intimately, each carrying its weight of truth and emotion.

From Nisha:

"Losing KK feels like a chapter of my life has closed too soon. I admired him for his kindness, simplicity, and unwavering support. He was someone I deeply liked and cared for, someone who brought light into my life in ways I didn't even realize at the time. His presence had a way of making everything feel easier, brighter, and more meaningful. Losing him felt like losing a part of myself—an emptiness that lingers despite the beautiful memories we created. He was not just someone I loved; he was a part of my journey, someone who taught me the true essence of connection and care. Even in his absence, he remains a part of me, etched forever in my heart."

– Nisha is an Assistant Manager of People Development and is happily married.

From Karuna:

"Love is the most powerful emotion. It can conquer hearts and transform souls. I shared my first love with KK—a love so innocent and pure that even after 20 years, it feels vivid in my memory. I still remember his heartfelt proposal, my acceptance, and the disapproval of my parents. When I realized they were unhappy, I chose to walk away and never look back.

But KK? He is truly a gem—a kind-hearted, loving, and compassionate person. He never forced me into anything, never burdened me with expectations. His love was pure, selfless, and maddeningly passionate. I regret breaking his heart, though it was never my intention to hurt him.

Even now, I cherish the memories we shared. KK taught me the meaning of unconditional love, and for that, I will always be grateful."

– Karuna is an English teacher by profession and happily married.

From Meher:

"The bond I share with KK, my best friend for life, is one of my most cherished possessions. His love was pure madness—unwavering, selfless, and untamed. While I saw him as a friend, KK was always there for me, no matter the circumstance. I still remember how he helped me during our exams, sacrificing his own preparation to ensure I understood the toughest concepts. He would sit with me for hours, patiently explaining everything until I felt confident.

Though I only saw him as a friend, I couldn't stand the thought of him being with someone else. There was something so genuine and irreplaceable about KK that made him impossible to let go of. He pushed me to be better, inspired me to grow, and never stopped believing in my potential.

Even today, KK and I remain each other's anchors. Whenever life gets tough, he's the first person I turn to, and I know he'll always be there. A best friend like KK is truly a rare gem, and I feel incredibly fortunate to have found him. To me, he's not just a friend—he's family, a part of my life I'll always treasure."

– Meher is happily married and a homemaker.

From Swati

Though they are no longer in touch, KK received a heartfelt e-card from Swati—a quiet yet powerful gesture that spoke volumes. In her message, she wrote:

I am sorry for everything that happened, KK. Life took us down different paths, but I want you to know that I hold no bitterness, only gratitude for the moments we shared. I will always pray for your happiness and hope you find all the peace and love you truly deserve.

It was a simple note, yet it carried the weight of reconciliation and unspoken emotions. For KK, it wasn't just an apology—it was a reminder that even the most broken ties can hold traces of care and compassion. Swati's words became a small yet significant part of KK's journey, one that reflected the beauty of letting go and wishing well.

– Swati is a faculty at a university and happily married.

From Samriddhi

Samriddhi and KK had lost touch over the years.

– Samriddhi is an Associate Experience Leader and happily married.

From Khushi:

Despite KK's attempts to reach out and share her story, Khushi remained silent. She chose not to comment, offering no words, no explanation, and no acknowledgment of their shared past. Perhaps silence, in her eyes, was the loudest statement she could make. In a way, KK understood—sometimes, the weight of the past is too heavy to speak about, and some chapters are meant to stay closed, even if they remain unfinished.

– Khushi is a Senior Manager and happy after the divorce.

"Love, it was never meant for me, a captive heart that longed to flee. It left no mark, no lasting trace, just empty skies and endless space."

* * * * *

Thanks To All My Readers

To all those who have read this book and walked with me through the pages of pain, hope, and resilience—thank you. Every word in this story was written from the heart, and I hope it has touched yours in some way. The road to healing is long and winding, but with love, friendship, and strength, we can conquer anything. Keep believing, keep fighting, and remember: sometimes, the most profound love comes in the form of those who never give up on you.

This book is dedicated to all the single parents, the warriors who fight every day to give their children a future filled with love and hope. You are the unsung heroes of this world.

www.ingramcontent.com/pod-product-compliance
Lightning Source LLC
LaVergne TN
LVHW041031150826
845672LV00001B/266

* 9 7 9 8 8 9 6 3 2 8 3 6 0 *